Hellfire

Hayley Briana

Hellfire

Hayley Briana

We all deserve someone who would walk through hellfire for us.

Note to the Reader

This work is a combination of The Hellfire Novellas. "Angel of Blood" and "Angel in Chains." More editing has been done on both novellas with additional content. Even if you have read the novellas you can still enjoy the bonus content in this book, though much will be similar.

This book contains explicit content and dark themes that may be considered traumatic and offensive to some readers.

For a full list of triggers, please visit the author's website HayleyBrianaWrites.com

Scan with your phone camera to see a full list of triggers

Playlist

Hellfire - Barns Courtney

Rest in Peace - Dorothy

Spider in the Roses - Sonia Leigh

I See Red - Everybody Loves an Outlaw

Teeth - 5 Seconds of Summer

Desire - Meg Myers

Killer - Valerie Broussard

Kiss or Kill - Stela Cole

The Devil Wears Lace - Steven Rodriguez

Slayer - Bruce Savage

PROLOGUE

"I'm not here to forgive you. Only your god can forgive you for the darkness of your soul."

Those were the last words he heard as the bullet met its mark between his eyes. His vacant eyes watched me as he crumbled to the floor. Another name off the list, and soon my ledger would drip red with their blood. I wouldn't stop until I had my revenge.

All that could be heard in this lonely church was the rain cascading down the stained-glass windows and the clack of my heels as I disappeared into the chilled night.

Onto the next, and last, target.

CHAPTER ONE

Angel

I was sitting on the fire escape of my crappy studio apartment. The rain was still coming down, but I just didn't care. I only had one last person to kill to avenge Jessica and he would be the hardest to get to. Especially with the other three dead and found murdered.

I tried to block out the memories that kept assaulting me tonight. You'd think it would be the fact I'd murdered someone in cold blood, but no. It was simply the face of Jessica with her fair skin and red hair laying in a heap, surrounded by a puddle of her own blood. Her face frozen in the terror of her last moments. All I could see was how her dress had been ripped from her body, hanging in tattered and bloody strips from her limbs. I wished all I could see was her beauty. Instead, I was haunted by that last image of her. When I found her dead in our home.

I was her older sister by two years. After we got out of the system, I failed her. Spending my life protecting her had taken a back seat. To give her a life I thought she deserved, I had been trying to earn enough for us to live comfortably. Working two jobs at the time hadn't been ideal, but someone needed to take care of her. She wanted to go to school, so I gave her that opportunity without the added worry of how to pay for it on top of our other bills. I should have paid more attention. I should have seen the signs and known when she started hanging around the less unsavory individuals at her school, especially at eighteen. They were the sort of people you didn't want to notice your existence, but she thrived on their attention. The bad boys loved her innocence. Someone who was easy to manipulate. She quickly became their favorite toy. I knew they were low-ranking members of the crew that ran the city. It soon became apparent that she was working her way up the ranks when she started bringing home expensive gifts. There was no way she could have afforded it on her own. I should have warned her, said something, but I was just too busy trying to keep the bills paid and her taken care of. I never thought I'd find her dead in our living room eight years ago.

I knew exactly who had been responsible for her death the day I found her. Previously, I'd scrounged up enough money to put a video security system in the house in case something were to happen. The footage showed every moment of what they'd done to her. The five men who pinned her to the ground as she tried to fight them off. How they'd torn her clothes to get to her and took turns forcing themselves on her. It hadn't mattered what part of her they had sunk their dicks into. All they cared about was taking from her and when they were done, her "boyfriend" stood up and put a bullet in her head. I'm sure it was over some petty jealously that she'd been fucking around on him, but that didn't warrant what they'd done to her.

The cops hadn't done shit, even though I had the evidence of what had occurred. They had the police department in their pocket, so nothing stuck. So it left me on my own to mourn the loss of my sister. I'd get justice for her if it was the last thing I did.

"Just one more Jessica. Those old bastards will get what they deserve." I whispered to the darkened sky before climbing back into my window.

I needed to get this blood washed off of me and get ready for surveillance by the next day. Jonathan, the little fucker I'd just killed in a church, had told me everything I needed to know to find his boss. I knew where I could find him now and how I was going to get close to him. Using his business against him, I was determined to catch his eye. Madax Ashford would regret the day he ever laid eyes on my sister.

I parked outside of the Hellfire club and watched as the line continued to grow outside. It was the hottest club in town, even though the majority didn't realize it was a front for the mafia that ran this city. It was owned by the boss's youngest son, Damon, and they had most of their underground meetings here. How the place had a clean record, I had no clue. The first thing I needed to do was get into the club, then I could work on the details of the plan to take down Madax.

Taking a deep breath, I climbed out of my black, beat-up 69 impala, adjusted my short dress, and made my way to the entrance. In this dress, I left little to the imagination, which would come in handy with the bouncer manning the door. It would grab the attention of most men if I set my sights on them. It was black, short, strapless showing off the ink covering my body. I had paired it with the tallest strappy red heels I'd ever owned. God, I hated this outfit. I hated the way heads turned as I approached the bouncer and as said man glanced my way; I gave him the most seductive smile I could muster.

"Sorry, beautiful, you'll have to wait in line like everyone else tonight." He said in a deep voice that sounded like he smoked three packs a day. He appeared fairly young, probably in his mid to late thirties, with the build of a lifter, a shaved head, and honey eyes. I could tell right away he used to be in the military.

"Oh, come on handsome, it can be our secret," I said to him, trailing my manicured nails up his muscular chest, "I can make it worth your while."

He seemed to contemplate for only a moment before going back to being stoic, "No can do. You'll have to wait in line like the others."

God, why couldn't he just make getting in easier for me? I forced myself to pout and run my eyes down his body. "Well, I guess it's your loss."

As I moved away from him to take a place in line outside the club, I heard the sexiest, deep tenor I'd ever had the pleasure of hearing, speaking from inside the door, "Ray, let her through."

I glanced over to see who had spoken and my breath caught. This man I recognized from my research and he could work to get what I wanted. Damon Ashford. The mafia prince himself was standing at the door in all his god-like glory. No man should ever look and sound like he did. He was at least 6'2", muscular in all the right places, covered in ink, with a well-groomed beard, long brown hair tied up into a messy bun, and steel-blue eyes that could bring any woman to her knees. He was bad news and could be a real problem if I didn't play my cards right.

I smiled his way, flipping my long, midnight hair over my shoulder, and sauntered up to him, "And who might I thank for saving me from waiting out in the cold?"

He flashed me a crooked smirk while lighting a cigarette. "Names Damon, and you?"

"Angel."

He let his steel eyes trail down my body and I could swear I felt the heat from his gaze like a caress. He was definitely going to be a problem. With a single glance, he could set my skin ablaze.

He puffed out a ring of smoke as his eyes met mine again and extended his arm to me. "Angel," He paused like he was savoring my name on his tongue, "let me buy you a drink."

It wasn't a question, and I didn't like the fact he thought he could boss me around. I fought the urge to glare at him and opted to simply smile up at him as he towered over me. "It would be my pleasure."

He finished his smoke and tossed the butt into a nearby ashtray before offering me his arm. I guess it was a plus that he didn't throw the damn things on the ground like most idiots. I timidly slipped my arm into his and let him escort me into the already packed club. Once we walked through the interior doors, I became slightly overwhelmed by the loud trap music and the smell of booze, smoke, and sweat. The neon and strobe lights were the only light within the entire club, other than those that lined the bar set against the sidewall as you entered the club. If Damon weren't escorting me, I probably would have spent most of the night searching for any sign of Madax in this damned crowd.

Damon led us straight to the bar and waved the bartender over.

"Damon, what can I get for you, sir?" The young man in his early twenties asked. He was blonde with a long, faded haircut. The top was long enough that the lengths fell over one of his green eyes. He was attractive and I could tell he used that to his advantage working in this club. Women were eyeing him almost as much as Damon. What was with the men who worked here being so attractive?

"Scotch, Zack," He said to the bartender before leaning in to whisper in my ear, "and you Angel?"

I felt myself shiver as his breath brushed my ear and neck. "Pomegranate martini, please."

Fuck, why was I having this reaction to a man I didn't know a thing about outside of his name and who his father was? He was the son of my target, and I needed to get my shit together. I needed to get away from him so I could do the job I set out to do. He ordered my drink and Zack got to work, making them as quickly as possible. Once he finished, he handed the drinks to Damon, who nodded for me to follow him through the crowd. He led me over to an empty plush sectional off to the side of the dance floor. He sat down, placing my drink on the table, leaned back, and crossed his ankle over the opposite knee.

I guess I would have to play nice for a bit. I took a seat next to him, maintaining a comfortable distance between us. Before crossing my legs, I grabbed my drink from the table, relaxing into the plush cushions.

"Thank you for getting me in and for the drink," I say politely while scanning the dance floor, acting as if I was looking for someone. I was hoping I would see Madax.

"My pleasure. Are you meeting someone here tonight?" He asks in a lazy tone.

"Just a few friends." I lie smoothly, glancing back over at him. "Why did you vouch to get me into the club?"

I needed to know what game he was playing, so I knew how I needed to proceed with this chance meeting.

"By the way you were sweet-talking the guy out front you seemed... desperate." He seemed to contemplate that last word.

I couldn't control my reaction to that comment and glared directly at him. "I've never been desperate for a day in my life."

Before he could reply, I stood and smiled in his direction. "Thanks again for the drink." I spoke in a clipped voice and walked away. I didn't have time to play with him when there was a much bigger fish to fry.

I spent the night wandering in the shadows of the club. Keeping an eye out for any sign of Madax. I had a feeling he was keeping to the upper levels, where I could see a mirrored wall above the dance floor. I confirmed my suspicion when a group of businessmen were escorted upstairs. Deciding that this wouldn't pan out the way I had planned, I would need to find a different way in. I finished my drink and made my way back to the bar. I waited to be served and smiled when Zack glanced my way. He smoothly slid a customer's drink across the bar to them before walking over to me.

"Another one for you, beautiful?" He smirked, taking my empty glass.

"Not this time, Zack, but you could tell a girl how she gets a job in a place like this," I said, giving him my most flirtatious smile.

"Oh, that's easy and as it just so happens, we are currently looking for a waitress. I'm in charge of the bar so I can hire you," he said with a wink. "Think you could start on Monday?"

"Monday would work out perfectly." Damn, that was much easier than I thought it would be. I could see just a hint of mischief in his gaze, so I knew that there had to be an ulterior motive for hiring me without so much as an interview.

Zack told me all the details of when to show up and that we can go over training before the weekend hits. I thanked him for the opportunity; we exchanged contact information, and I quickly slipped out of the club. Now that I had a way to get into the club regularly, I also had a way to get close to the bastard who killed my sister.

CHAPTER TWO

Damon

I watched as the little Angel wandered off to disappear into the crowd with a confident grin. I had a gut feeling that she was hiding something, and I wanted to know what it was. It had been a while since anyone had caught my interest.

Once I'd lost sight of her in the crowd, I stood from my spot and made my way to the VIP section on the upper level of the club. The guards let me in and the room immediately became quiet when the door shut behind me. It was a soundproofed room that housed a private bar and sitting area. The far wall overlooked the club with a floor-to-ceiling window, which I silently walked over to and glanced out. Looking for a certain dark-haired beauty.

My father was sitting on the couch with a phone to his ear, discussing a new business deal. Who knew what about at this point? He had his fingers in every dirty pot in the city; from drugs to the skin trade. I had never been a fan of all his methods for running the business. The old fuck needed to just give Dimitri control because he was fucking up the reputation of the family name.

He hung up the phone and walked over next to me. I could smell his expensive cologne and it made me sick. Like he was trying to cover up the rot inside of him despite being in excellent health, sadly.

"How are things on the ground tonight?" He asked as he took a swig from his tumbler.

"Things are fine. No fights have broken out, and the bar is running smoothly. I'm still looking for someone to help with the bar. It's far too busy for just Zack and Cherry. How's *business*?"

He glanced my way from the corner of his eye, but I paid him no mind. "Expanding."

That could only mean that the call was about finding new "recruits" for the skin trade. It was the one part of the business that none of us ever agreed on. Even Dimitri hated it. Regardless of the money it brought in, once Dimitri and I took over, it would be the first thing to go. We may run the city and it's underground, but that was a level of debauchery I would never sink to.

"Go enjoy yourself tonight, son. I have no use for you this evening." He spoke with authority as he walked over to the private bar to refill his glass.

It was his way of dismissing me prior to his associates showing up. They planned to discuss using the club as a front to find more girls to fill their empty slots for market. Just the thought had me wanting to blow his brains across the wall. This was my bar, but until he was out of the picture, I had to follow orders. I'd soon kill this fucker, and those he did business with. He trained me to be a ruthless killer and I would enjoy the day I got to be his executioner.

I nodded in his direction, "Yes, sir," and walked out of the stuffy room.

I would much rather find Angel. She was going to be a fun little distraction. I wanted to see just how dark she could get. I'd leave Dimitri to deal with our father for the evening.

Making my way around the club, it disappointed me to not find a single glimpse of Angel, so I went straight to the heart of gossip, Zack. He was sliding drinks from one end of the bar to the other. How he and Cherry handled that bar alone, I would never understand. I slipped behind the bar and got to work helping him trim the herd down so that we could speak.

Once there were only a handful of people left at the bar, Zack turned to me with a raised brow, wiping his hands on a towel.

"What's up boss?" He was always so easygoing and to the point.

"Have you seen the girl I came in with earlier?" I asked as I wiped up the bar top.

"Oh, you mean Angel? Yeah, she swung back by the bar about 10 minutes ago before she left. Was asking about getting a job, so I hired her on as a waitress."

I couldn't help but grin in his direction. Of course, he'd just hire a pretty girl with no questions asked. I adored the fucker, but he had a tendency to get himself into trouble with the ladies. This did, however, make it much easier to track her down.

"When will she be starting?" I tossed the dirty towel into the wastebasket and poured myself another drink.

"Monday. Figured I'd show her the ropes before throwing her to the wolves during the weekend rush." He said, leaning against the bar, his eyes roaming across the busy floor. The horny bastard was probably looking for his next conquest.

"Sounds good." I downed my tumbler and walked off, giving him a slight wave of thanks.

CHAPTER THREE

Angel

The weekend came and went. Today was officially my first day working at the club. I opted for a casual look of a black cut-up tee that showed off just the right amount of cleavage, short daisy dukes, and thigh-high combat boots with my hair pulled up in a loose ponytail. I quickly lined my eyes in a black liner that smudged slightly, giving a not-so-put-together smokey eye, some simple mascara, and topped it off with a bold, red lip stain. Checking to make sure I had my phone and keys, and slipped my needlepoint knife into the side of my boot before heading out to the club.

Because it was a Monday afternoon, the bar was mostly empty outside of some staff and vendors. Zack waved me over when he saw me walk inside. He was sitting at the bar eating a bowl of peanuts, while Damon was standing next to him signing the paperwork of a vendor. I smiled and made my way over.

Before coming in, I looked up all I could about the club. Damon was the owner of the place and he had built it from the ground up two years ago at age 36. His father and brother were big investors in the club and did most of their business here. It was a hot spot for club-goers on the weekend and had been kept squeaky clean, at least to the eyes of the public.

Damon watched me closely as I made my way over to them, and I simply smiled as I took a seat next to Zack. I turned away from him and started talking with Zack about all the duties I'd have, the hours to expect, and just the basics of starting a new job. He even went as far as demanding that I understand that the door to the basement in the back was completely off-limits to anyone who wasn't management. Once he finished explaining everything, he gave me an apron and put me to work behind the bar, making a variety of drinks to test my skills.

He watched me closely as he tossed peanuts into his mouth.

"Boss, I think we have a natural on our hands." He said, turning to Damon.

"Appears so, make me a Blue Blazer, if you will." Damon had a challenge in his eyes and it was obvious why. A Blue Blazer could be a complicated drink. I was learning, however, that the man before me was a lover of scotch.

"Coming right up, Mr. Ashford," I said, getting to work boiling some water and placing two glass mugs inside.

"Come on, man, you just have to test her with the fancy stuff, don't you?" I heard Zack say to Damon with a hint of worry in his voice.

Once the glasses were heated, I tossed the water and boiled the additional water I'd need. Laying a damp hand towel on the bar, I got to work mixing the new boiled water, scotch, and sugar into one mug. Lighting a match, I was careful to ignite the mixture, and transfer it from cup to cup before evening out both mugs, and extinguishing the flames. I topped each glass with a lemon twist. Sliding the drinks over to Damon and Zack, I flashed them a proud smile and waited for the final verdict.

They shared a silent glance before taking a swig from their mugs.

"Holy shit, this is good." Zack praised while taking another drink.

Damon eyed me as he swished the drink in the mug. I swear those steel eyes could see right through me, and I knew I'd have to be careful around him. It was obvious I intrigued him, although he didn't trust me. It's a good thing he wasn't the one I was after.

"Good start, Angel, but let's see how you do under pressure when the club's packed." He gave a crooked smirk before walking off. I couldn't help but watch him as he left. He had a nice firm ass and his muscles strained against his tight-fitted gray t-shirt. He was a god among men and I'd have had to be blind not to stare.

"Just ignore him. He's an asshole most of the time." Zack said, handing me back his empty mug and peanut bowl.

I went about cleaning up my area and washing the few dirty dishes. "He doesn't seem too bad."

"You say that now. Just wait until you get to know him better." A smirk graced his lips, and I had a feeling he wanted me to get to know our boss *much* better. Was that his plan all along?

About the time I finished cleaning up, a blonde girl with a bubbly personality skipped up to the bar and sat next to Zack.

"Hey Zacky! Is this the new girl? Hi, it's nice to meet you. I'm Cherry, the only other waitress in this place." She giggled. Though she was peppy, I could tell I'd enjoy working with her.

"Names Angel. It's a pleasure to meet you, Cherry." I smiled her way as I put away all the clean supplies.

Cherry and Zack showed me the ropes of everything I'd be doing once the bar opened and we spent the day getting ready for the evening crowd. They assured me that weeknights would be slow and then Friday things would get a lot more chaotic. I just hoped that this work would pay off in the end.

The week at the club flew by and I found that not once had I seen any of the Ashford family. To say it disappointed me was an understatement, but hopefully, they would show up this weekend. Most of the club running seemed to be left to Zack during the slow weeks. I got ready in my usual attire that had just become my normal, only topping it off with a black leather jacket to fight off the autumn evening chill before heading out to my night shift at the club.

I waved to Ray on my way into the club and he gave me a slight nod, as had become the norm during my first week. I came to learn a lot about the little staff of the Hellfire Club. There were very few of us. Zack was 23 and had been working here alongside his twin sister Chery since they had turned 21. Apparently, they had been family friends of the Ashford boys their entire lives and when Damon built the club; he asked them to work for him to help run the place. Ray was the quiet, broody type and was an ex-marine. I got the vibe that he had, had his hands bloodied on many accounts, and didn't want to be on his bad side. He kept his head shaved with just a slight bit of stubble along his square jaw. He was only a few years younger than Damon, and they had grown up together as well. It was more of a family dynamic and I was going to have to play it safe to stay on everyone's good side while I snooped around.

They weren't kidding about the club turning to chaos on Friday. Only thirty minutes into making it in for my shift, the club was packed full while trap music blasted through the speakers. The dance floor was covered in sweaty bodies grinding against one another while I slipped around the crowd, taking orders and delivering drinks. The night was a blur of work and at about midnight I was beat. I placed some dirty glasses in the sink behind the bar and got to washing everything.

"Hey Angel, after you finish that, head upstairs and take a break. You've been working your ass off tonight." Zack said, giving me a wink.

"I don't know how you and Cherry handled all this on your own. It's a madhouse."

He shrugged. "It keeps you busy, and you get used to it."

I finished drying the dishes and putting them away before heading off to the break room on the top floor.

The best part, it was right next to the private VIP lounge where I knew the Ashfords had most of their *business meetings*. I had seen Damon, Madax, and a tall man in a suit enter that room at the start of the night. To my surprise, as I made my way to the break room, the door wasn't guarded and had been left open a crack. I slipped up next to it to listen to the conversation going on inside.

"I don't give a shit what you two think. This is my business, and it's time you both learned your place. You don't have control of the business *yet*." A gruff voice shouted. It was aged, so I knew it had to be Madax.

"We simply don't think that market is a good look for business, sir." A calm voice, dripping with authority, spoke. That had to be the man in the suit I'd seen, the oldest Ashford son, Dimitri.

"It's good money and it'll give us more pull in other business ventures. It's already decided and I won't hear another word against it."

I heard Damon's deep scoff. He obviously wasn't happy with the choice of whatever "market" was. I decided now wasn't the best time to be snooping and slipped away, heading into the break room. I quickly made myself a cup of coffee and relaxed on the little couch for a bit, scrolling through my phone. So far, working here has not given me much to go on. I'd need to gain these people's trust so that I could get closer to Madax. It seemed the only people that could get close were his sons, his business associates who visited the club, and Cherry, on occasions when she would take drinks up to the VIP lounge and quickly be dismissed.

The door to the break room swung open, hitting the doorjamb with a loud thud. I glanced over to see Damon stomp in like he was pissed at the world. He didn't even pay me any mind as he walked over to the counter to make himself a cup of coffee.

"Bad night, boss?" I asked, going back to scrolling on my phone.

"Same shit, different day. Why are you up here instead of working?" He said, leaning against the counters and taking a sip of his coffee. Tonight, he was in a black button-up dress shirt that had 3 top buttons undone at the top, black dress slacks, shiny leather oxford shoes, and his long hair tied up in a messy bun. Fuck, it should be illegal to look that good.

"Things slowed down a bit, so Zack told me to come take a break." I glanced back his way and admired how his chest tattoos peeked out from the gap of his shirt.

How I'd like to run my tongue along those designs. I'd never laid eyes on a more attractive man in my life. I had to slap myself mentally to get my head straight. He's the fucking enemy and I wouldn't let him get in my way of revenge.

He seemed to watch me just as intently as his eyes ran along my exposed legs. We continued to sit in silence, just taking each other in until he finally spoke again. "I get the feeling you are hiding something, little Angel."

I scoffed, standing up to wash my mug in the sink next to him. "Isn't everyone hiding something?"

"Fair point."

Standing this close to him, his scent filled my senses, and I squeezed my thighs together, heat pooling at my core. It was a heady mix of mahogany with a hint of something sweet, like apples. What the fuck was wrong with me when he was around? It was this insane pull that I was helpless to resist and it did nothing except piss me off and leave me feeling distracted. I quickly washed my cup and sat it to the side of the dish drainer.

As soon as I'd placed the cup down, a hand wrapped around the front of my throat and pinned me to the wall next to the sink. I gasped in surprise and slipped my knife out of my boot, holding it to Damon's throat as he pinned me. He just smirked down at me, his blue eyes shining with a warning.

"I wouldn't do that if I were you, Angel." He said in his smooth, deep voice. I could feel his breath on my face with a hint of cigarette smoke and scotch.

I bared my teeth at him, pressing the knife harder against his throat. "Then I suggest you get your hands off me."

"And I suggest you keep your nose out of other people's business." Shit, he knew I had been spying on them.

He released my throat, backing away, and I slipped my knife back into my boot. I felt his eyes watching my every move, and it set my skin on fire. He was so much more observant than I gave him credit for. I needed to get done with this job and scatter as quickly as possible.

"Back to work. I hope the rest of your night goes better." I said, walking out without glancing his way.

CHAPTER FOUR

Damon

Sitting in this room with my father and Dimitri was the last place I wanted to be. Father was going on about how he was going to use the club to find fresh recruits for his business partner, and it was pissing me off. Like hell, if he was going to get away with fucking with my club. Dimitri sat on the sofa next to me, running his hands through his hair. A habit he had for whenever he was feeling stressed or frustrated. We were on the same page as far as my father working with the skin trade.

I sat silently, knowing that if I went off, I'd put a bullet in the old fuck's head. Glancing towards the door, I saw a head of black hair slip by the gap in the door. It seemed the little angel was a nosy little thing.

"I'd rather not have that sort of *business* around my club. I've done my best to keep this a legitimate club outside of you meeting your people here." I meant for the statement to come out calm, but I wasn't Dimitri, and it sounded more like a growl even to my own ears.

Father's glare turned directly to me as his face turned a slightly darker shade of red. "You wouldn't have this dump if it wasn't for me. I let you build it because I thought giving you something to focus on would keep you from fucking up the business. I'll do with this building as I see fit."

I clenched my fist, ready to jump off the couch and pummel the old man. Before I could inch forward off the couch, Dimitri placed a calming hand on my shoulder. The bastard knew that the old man would deserve it and he was still holding me back. I guess that was why he was the brains and knew how to handle our father in his own element. I'd always been the troublemaker who got into fights, while Dimitri was always calm and strategized every single move he made. Sometimes I was envious of his calm, like right now.

"We understand where you are coming from, sir, but Damon has worked hard to build this place up and it brings in a large percentage of our profits. However, Damon makes a fair point that this is a clean business. Maybe it would be best that your partners scout out the club for potential stock, but they follow them to an off-site location. This ensures they get what they want and Damon's business can't be tied to the girl's disappearances." Dimitri spoke fluidly with a matter-of-fact air about him. It still pissed me off that the shitbag thought he could just use my club whenever he wanted. Fuck him and fuck this.

"That seems reasonable. I will let my associates know the details."

At that, I got up and stormed out, heading to the break room in the next room. All I wanted to do was break something or make someone bleed. When was Dimitri going to give me the okay to kill the old fucker already? I know he was doing things behind the scenes, but I was tired of waiting around. I slung open the door to the break room and was surprised to see Angel laying on the couch on her phone. She glanced my way, and I pretended not to notice her as I made my way over to the coffeemaker to pour myself a cup.

"Bad night, boss?" Her soft, husky voice asked from behind me. The sound was like fucking music to my ears.

"Same shit, different day. Why are you up here instead of working?" I asked, despite knowing she hadn't had a break all evening. The club was packed, and it was her first-weekend shift.

She seemed to have a hard time keeping her eyes in one place, glancing between me and her phone as I leaned back against the countertop. I watched her face as her eyes roamed my body, setting me on fire with her scorching blue eyes. So cold they burned like ice.

"Things slowed down a bit, so Zack told me to come take a break." She said in the most seductively sweet voice I'd ever heard. I had a feeling she didn't even have to try getting a man's attention with a body and voice like that. I hadn't paid it much mind, but the girl was covered in ink. It covered every exposed area of skin I could see and, from the looks of it, they disappeared into much more interesting places. Thorny rose vines were wrapping up both her legs while snakes slithered up each one hidden in the foliage, heading in the direction I'd love to trail my hands.

We stayed silent as we both took each other in until I spoke. "I get the feeling you are hiding something, little Angel."

She scoffed, and I had to hide my grin behind my coffee mug as she stood, walking over to the sink next to me to wash out her empty cup. "Isn't everyone hiding something?"

This woman was much more observant than I gave her credit for. I knew she was sticking around for something. I just needed to find out what. Thankfully, a guy owed me a favor and was looking into her, "Fair point."

I eyed her tense figure as she washed her cup. Standing this close, I could just make out the faint scent of lavender and lilac, which seemed to draw me into her like a fly caught in a web. I wanted to bend her over this counter and fuck her wet cunt. I was positive she'd be soaking wet for me. She placed her cup in the drainer and I immediately wrapped my hand around her throat, forcing her against the wall. What I didn't expect was her holding a knife to my throat in the same instant, her back hit the wall. I couldn't help the sensation that raced through me as I grinned at her, my dick straining against the zipper of my pants. This bitch had a fire in her and I wanted to watch it burn. To let it consume me.

"I wouldn't do that if I were you," I said as she pressed the blade harder against my throat, just enough to let me know she was serious, but not to draw blood.

She bared her teeth at me like a caged animal, and a fire ignited behind those blue eyes. "Then I suggest you get your hands off me."

I grinned, knowing just how I could get her flustered. "And I suggest you keep your nose out of other people's business."

Her eyes rounded in shock and I could feel her heartbeat skyrocket along my fingers that wrapped around her throat and what a pretty throat it was, too. I had a feeling Angel would love being choked while I fucked her. She wasn't scared to fight back, which made me positive she'd be just as vicious in the sack.

I released her throat and backed away from her. Giving her some space before I took her right here in this room, whether she wanted it or not. I watched as she slipped her knife back into her boot before she straightened. She wouldn't even meet my eyes now.

"Back to work. I hope the rest of your night goes better." She said, walking out of the room without looking back.

I would most definitely be having a better night because I fully intended to end my night between those gorgeous thighs of hers. Until then, though, I needed to take care of my issue before heading back to get more business taken care of.

As quickly as I could, I shut and locked the door before undoing my pants. I was rock hard and throbbing for Angel. I wrapped my hand around the length and envisioned it was her mouth sliding along my cock. With the image of her on her knees before me and my hand creating a fast pace, I pleasured myself to the image that would be burned into my brain. Fuck her and my reaction to her. Still, I growled out her name as my release coated my hand. I couldn't wait to claim my little angel.

Hellfire had just closed, and the crew was cleaning up after a successful evening. I had slipped off to my office in the back of the club to get some last-minute paperwork done when my cell began vibrating in my pocket. I quickly fished it out, glancing at the restricted number that popped up.

"What do you have for me, Jensen?" I said, setting the paperwork to the side.

"Angel Hart, 28, was placed into the system with her younger sister at age 11. Once aging out, she took on the role of guardian for her sister, Jessica. They moved here into a small apartment 8 years ago until her sister was found murdered in their home. There were no leads, and it was labeled a cold case. Looks like someone did a marvelous job of covering shit up, you know, besides leaving the body. Since then, she's been holding odd jobs throughout the city and never seems to stay in the same place for long. She has no other records and little else is known about her. I can do some more digging if it is needed."

"Did the sister have the same last name?" I asked, lighting a cigarette and leaning back in my chair.

I heard the stroke of keys over the line before Jensen spoke again. "Jessica Murphy. Their mother was a common hooker, so they had different fathers. The fathers were never a part of their lives and their mother died from a drug overdose."

Well, that was an interesting turn of events. I recall a girl named Jessica being brought around with my father. She was young and impressionable. I wasn't sure what had happened when she just stopped showing up. The fact she had been murdered gave me a pretty good idea that my father had been involved. Was that why Angel was here? This could come in handy, if so. She could be an important part of our plans to get rid of the old fuck and take over the business.

"Thanks, Jensen," I said, hanging up the phone before he could even reply.

Standing from behind my desk, I decided on going out back to give Dimitri a call. I needed his opinion on if I should confront her. He would be much more level-headed than me. I slipped out the back door while dialing his number. When he answered, I gave him the rundown of the information Jensen had pulled up on her.

"She could be useful if it's not a coincidence that she's now working at your club. We could have her do the dirty work and we keep our hands clean," He sighed into the receiver before continuing, "Some of Father's more unsavory business partners have been reported murdered. There is no evidence or connection between them. I doubt that one woman could have taken them all out."

I grinned around my cigarette and recalled her holding that knife to my throat. "I think she might surprise you, brother."

"You find out more about her and we can go from there." I could almost hear the eye roll in his voice before he disconnected the call.

I leaned against the rough brick in the shadows, tossing my cigarette onto the pavement, when the back door to the club opened and out walked Angel with a bag of trash. I watched from the shadows as she tossed the bag into the dumpster, before walking back towards the door. However, I didn't intend on her making it that far just yet.

CHAPTER FIVE

Angel

It had been a long night. Not only had it been busy, but the encounter with Damon had been on my mind for most of the evening. I couldn't get rid of the tingling sensation of his hand on my throat. I was just ready to get home at this point. Walking out back, the cold air hits me, sending a chill down my spine. The alley behind the club was completely dark, with only the light of the moon to illuminate the shiny dumpster. After tossing the bag of trash into the dumpster, I headed back to the back door. As I was about to reach for the handle, I felt a presence behind me and in the blink of an eye, my front was pressed to the dirty brick wall. I quickly went into fight mode, trying to push away from the wall to get away from whoever this asshole was. I felt the warm breath of the person on my neck and was overwhelmed with a sweet mahogany scent and scotch.

"What the fuck do you think you're doing, Damon?" I growled between clenched teeth. I could feel the hard planes of his muscular body pressed against my back and everywhere our bodies connected, my skin grew heated.

He slipped his hand into the hair at the nape of my neck, gripping tightly and jerking my head back so that I was forced to look up at him. He had a mischievous smirk on his face that I really just wanted to stab with my knife.

"I just wanted to talk to you. I found some interesting information I thought you might help me with."

I just glared at him as he pressed himself harder against my back. This bastard was playing games I wasn't interested in playing. "What do you want?"

"I want to know why you are really here, Angel. Does it have something to do with my father's connection to Jessica?" He said as he held his face in my hair.

I felt myself hold my breath as my heart rate increased. How had he fucking figured that out? If he knew what I was up to, I was as good as dead. I refused to be taken out before I finished what I had started. I moved my hand down to my knife, ready to fight my way out of this if I had to. Before my hand could wrap around the hilt, his free hand gripped my wrist, and he tsked at me like he was scolding a child.

"That's not very nice, Angel," He slipped his hand lower, removing my knife and dragging the sharp edge up along my thigh, "I was hoping we could help each other."

The sensation of the knife and his breath along my neck was wreaking havoc on my mind. I didn't like the reactions he had on my body. "I don't know what you're talking about." Hissing, I pushed back against him.

I could feel him smile against me as he tossed the knife to the side, replacing it with his rough, callused hands. Goosebumps broke across my skin and my breath hitched slightly.

"Don't play dumb, Angel. You're smarter than that."

He slipped his hand from my thigh to in between my legs, running his fingers along my covered slit. When his fingers pressed firmly to my clit, my body automatically responded by grinding harder into his hand. What the fuck was wrong with me?

He chuckled at my reaction to his ministrations and began working the throbbing bundle of nerves through my shorts. A breathy moan slipped from my lips and my thoughts scattered. I didn't know what power he had over me, but I couldn't stop my reactions. Warnings blared in my ears that I should fight back. He was onto me and I needed to get away from him.

"Tell me the truth Angel, then I'll make you come harder than you ever have in your life." He growled deeply as he continued to pleasure me with his fingers.

Without thinking, the words spilled from my lips, "I want him dead."

"Good girl," He removed his hands from my aching core and spun me to face him, pinning my arms at my sides, "consider it done."

I stared at him in complete shock. I just confessed to wanting to kill his father, and he had agreed. It couldn't be that simple. This had to be some sort of sick game. His hands slipped from my arms, one wrapping around my throat, while the other worked on the buttons of my shorts. He slipped his hand inside and growled as he felt my wet center. My body had a mind of its own where he was concerned.

"So wet for me, Angel." He nearly purred as his fingers slipped inside of me while the palm of his hand worked my clit and I gripped the wrist around my throat. I bit my lip, trying to stifle the moans, wanting to slip past.

He continued to work my center until I could feel my walls gripping his fingers. I was so close already. He moved his hand into my hair as he crashed his mouth to mine. It was a hungry sort of kiss, and he was completely in control. I gripped his broad shoulders to steady myself as I kissed him back, biting and nipping at his lips and tongue. Moaning into his mouth as I came apart on his hand. As soon as the waves of pleasure had passed, he removed his hand from my shorts and slipped back into the club, leaving me breathless, leaning against the wall. What had just happened?

As soon as I got back to my crappy apartment, I collapsed onto my bed. The metal frame squeaked loudly in the small space. I couldn't get the night and everything that had happened with Damon out of my head. My body was on fire from his touch.

I had attempted to find him once I had gained my composure, but Zack said he had already left for the night. I needed to find out why he had acted the way he did. Why manipulate me into telling him my goal and then touch me the way he did? What game was he playing at?

The questions filled my mind as I lay there trying to get to sleep. I would have to confront him tomorrow if he was at the club. When it was obvious, I wasn't getting any sleep. I got up and turned on some crappy TV show to clear my head.

I awoke with a start when there was a knock on my door. Glancing at the time on my phone, seeing it was just past noon. I must have fallen asleep last night while watching TV. Slipping off the couch, I decided it was best to see what was at the door. Doing so, I found a bouquet of red roses on my welcome mat. I looked around to see the hallway empty before picking up the flowers and shutting the door behind me. Walking into my small kitchen area, I sat the roses down, fishing out the card to see who they were from.

I can't wait to see you tonight. -D

I scoffed, rolling my eyes and tossing the card on the counter. I needed to figure out what he was planning so that I could make sure I came out on top.

Deciding it was probably best to shower and get ready for my shift at Hellfire. Taking my time to shower, applying light smokey makeup, and tossing on a pair of ripped jeans along with a black, strappy crop top. Tonight, I would wear my knife in my thigh holster, so that it was easier to get to in case I ended up needing it. I had a feeling death was stalking me at the moment and I wouldn't go down without a fight.

Once I was ready, I decided I was going to take my bike instead of the car today. I admired her before climbing on. It had taken me a while to save up for her, but her smooth riding was well worth it. A blacked-out 2016 Harley-Davidson Breakout. I always loved how freeing it felt to ride her down the winding roads outside of the city. As soon as all this was over, I planned to hop on my bike and ride to wherever the road took me. As far from my bloody past as possible.

CHAPTER SIX

Damon

Zack was running me through the weekly drink specials he had come up with when I saw Angel walk through the front door. She held a bike helmet under her arm as she made her way over. I didn't take her as the type to be into riding, but the thought of her straddling my bike had my cock straining against my jeans.

I appeared to be listening intently to Zack rather than watching her slip behind the bar. She was in a crop top and ripped jeans today. I had to admit I loved her casual attire and the way her jeans hugged her curvaceous ass.

"Sounds good, Zack," I said in approval before turning my gaze fully toward Angel.

"Hey there, Angel," I smirked her way, dragging my eyes down to her figure.

I noticed a slight dusting of color along her cheeks as she nodded toward me, slipping her helmet into a cabinet under the bar. Zack simply glanced between us like he could feel the tension in the air. He cleared his throat before announcing that he was going to the back to grab some extra bottles. Once he was gone, I got up from my stool at the bar and walked over to where Angel was getting things straightened out before the night began. Was she purposely trying to avoid looking at me? That just wouldn't do.

I approached her from behind and caged her in against the bar with my arms on either side of her. She tensed as her hands paused from where she was whipping the bar in front of her.

"What are you playing at, Damon?" She asked in that sultry voice I loved, just barely above a whisper.

"I believe I made that perfectly clear last night," I breathed against the back of her neck, watching her shiver,

"We both want my father dead. I believe we can help each other."

She glanced at me over her shoulder. "And what about the rest?"

I couldn't help the grin that graced my lips. I couldn't get the little sounds she made as she came apart on my hand last night out of my head. She could have stopped me easily, instead she had let me bring her pleasure. I'd be the first to admit I had to fuck my hand three times before I could even think of sleeping. I couldn't stay away from her and I knew that the fact that I affected her was something she wasn't the happiest about. Instead of answering her question, I simply pushed away from the bar and began my way to the office in the back.

She would get answers tonight when Dimitri got the chance to speak with her. Until then, she'd simply have to deal with the unanswered questions. The business side of things was easy. Dimitri would take care of making the plan while I was sure Angel and I would handle the dirty details. It was the draw to her I wasn't sure about. She was a challenge for me, and I wanted to break her in the most pleasurable ways possible. I wanted her to bleed so beautifully for me.

CHAPTER SEVEN

Angel

It was another busy night, with Saturday being much busier than the night before. Cherry was helping Zack behind the bar while I was maintaining orders for the floor and VIP areas. We worked our asses off serving drinks and appetizers through the night and I couldn't help the sigh of relief once we had closed up. Damon had even disappeared after that first encounter of the evening.

I sat down at the bar, downing a glass of water while Zack was finishing up inventory for the night. "So, where did Cherry disappear to?"

"She slipped upstairs to see Dimitri." Zack said, throwing a wink over his shoulder.

I was surprised. From what I had seen of Dimitri, he was the calm businessman type, whereas Cherry was bubbly and a ray of sunshine. It may have made sense if the whole 'opposites attract' thing was something to be believed.

We had finished everything up for closing by the time Cherry made her way back to us. She skipped her way over to the bar and took a seat next to me.

"The boys want to see you back in the office?" She said with a sweet smile and a wink.

"Uh oh, sounds like someone is in trouble." Zack taunted with a grin as he ate his hundredth bowl of peanuts of the night. The boy had a strange addiction to the damn things.

I just rolled my eyes at both of them and made my way toward the back office. Once I made it to the door, I rapped my knuckles on the red oak door a few times.

"Come in, Angel." I heard Damon growl from the other side of the door. The tenor of his voice sent shivers down my spine.

I opened the door and walked in to find Dimitri sitting behind the desk, running his hands through his dark hair. He looked like the weight of the world rested on his shoulders and had a permanent scowl on his face. It was still so hard to imagine him and the bubbly Cherry together. Damon was leaning against the edge of the desk with a cigarette held between his teeth as he flashed me a crooked smirk. I quickly glanced away from him and focused on Dimitri.

"Let's get this over with, shall we?" I spoke with more confidence than I felt as I took a seat in front of them. To keep my hands busy, I took out my knife and began cleaning my nails with it.

Dimitri was the first to speak up, folding his hands in front of himself on the desk. "I need to know everything. What you have planned, why you're after our father, everything, Ms. Hart."

I took the chance to glance at Damon from the corner of my eye before focusing back on Dimitri, laying my knife on the desk in front of me. "Your father's responsible for the rape and murder of my younger sister. I planned on getting close to him and killing him. It's as simple as that."

"And is that why you killed all those other men, Angel?" Damon spoke as he put out his cigarette in a nearby ashtray.

"Yes," was my simple answer. I wasn't showing these guys any fear. I wasn't scared of them. If they had wanted me dead, they would have done it by now. Made it look like an accident.

"I want to know the details of those other deaths." Dimitri said, grabbing my attention again.

I recounted the death of every man I had killed so far. Explaining how I'd used my body to my advantage and took them out as soon as I got any needed information out of them. I explained what had happened to Jessica and how her "boyfriend" had been the first man I had killed in order to find out all the names of those involved in her murder. I even went as far as showing them the footage I'd saved from our security system. They didn't even make it a few minutes into the video before cutting it off and handing the phone back. The shit was sick, so I completely understood their reaction.

It was odd telling these two all the gory details of my life following the day I walked in to find my sister's mutilated body. It felt freeing to finally talk to someone about it. I had no family, no friends, and had been utterly alone for the past eight years. It was as if a weight had been lifted from me, but I still had to remain cautious. I couldn't exactly trust these two.

It became clear who the man in charge was, so I focused all my attention on Dimitri. He was going to be the one who determined my fate. "What reason would you have to talk to me rather than kill me? Madax is your father, regardless of what he's done, and he's essentially your boss."

"We want the old fuck dead as much as you do, Angel," Damon said as he plopped down in a chair next to me.

I kept quiet, waiting for him or Dimitri to elaborate, "He's destroying the business slowly and we've lost credibility with many of our former partners. Not everyone in the underground is interested in working with human trafficking. They are pulling their funds and siding with our competitors. We have been biding our time, waiting for the best moment to take him out so that we can take over the business." Dimitri said as he watched me closely.

"And what does this have to do with me?"

"We want you to be the one to end him. Essentially, you get your revenge and we keep our hands clean. We will help you as needed to get close to him. However, I have some things to work out before he can be eliminated." Dimitri leveled me with a glare before standing up to pour himself a glass of scotch across the room.

"What you mean is that if I am caught, I go down," I state, glancing between the two brothers.

Damon just grinned as he eyed me, and Dimitri pretended like I was simply an inconvenience. I got the feeling he didn't like or trust me very much. Good, at least he wasn't stupid.

"Okay, I'm in. Now, how do you intend to get me close to Madax?" I asked.

CHAPTER EIGHT

Damon

After agreeing to work with us, Dimitri explained how Angel could get close to our shit bag father. He instructed her to take Cherry's place serving in the VIP lounge, where my father planned to have a meeting. We'd spent the entire week preparing her, though I knew she'd do things her own way. She was a fucking minx who didn't take orders well. Once her mind was made up, she wouldn't stop until she got what she wanted. I couldn't wait to see her in action tonight.

I watched her as she worked the crowd. She'd decided on a short skirt and crop top for tonight as she served and took orders down below on the main floor.

Those thigh-high boots made her long legs even more delectable. I wasn't happy that she planned to seduce my father. I wanted her attention on me, but I knew I couldn't let my possessiveness get in the way. This plan had to work. My father and his business partners would arrive soon and I'd get to see her in action, but I wanted her to myself before their arrival. I made a call down to the bar, asking Zack to send her up with some drinks to start the night.

I continued to watch her as she worked before making her way to the bar. She was speaking to Zack and handed her orders off to Cherry before glancing up at the window to the lounge. Even though I knew she couldn't see me, it was as if she was staring right at me. I felt my cock hardening against my slacks as I watched her make her way upstairs with a tray of bottles and empty glasses.

When she walked into the room, I had already taken a seat on a sofa as she began setting everything out on the private bar. She was so much fun to watch as she made a glass of scotch before making her way over to me. The way she walked was sensual, with little effort on her part. She bent down to place the tumbler on the glass table in front of me, and I couldn't help but to slide my hand up her thigh to her luscious ass. It was round and fit perfectly in my hands. Hooking my other hand around the opposite thigh, I pulled her towards me, forcing her to straddle my lap. She was tense, but I could see the hunger in those cold eyes of hers.

"What do you want, Damon?" She sounded absolutely bored. I wasn't sure if she was trying to convince me or herself at this point that she didn't want me.

"I just wanted to see what you had on underneath this little skirt of yours," I said as I slipped my finger underneath her lacy thong, running my fingers lightly along her slit until I was at her wet, hot center.

I inserted a finger, fucking her slowly as her breath caught. "So wet for me, Angel."

"I'm just excited about tonight." She gasped as she gripped tighter onto my shoulders.

I smirked, adding a second figure into her wet cunt. "So the idea of killing a man makes you this wet?"

Her only response was a breathy moan as I curved my fingers to rub that sensitive little spot inside of her. She ground her hips, trying to get more friction where she needed it. This was going to be a fun little game of getting her to admit that she wanted me. My Angel was stubborn.

I quickly flipped her over onto the couch, pinning her down with my free hand as I kissed my way down her throat. She pushed against me as if her fight was restored, which just made me pin her down harder. Removing my fingers from her dripping wet cunt, I gripped the crotch of her thong, ripping the flimsy fabric from her body. She gasped, pausing in her fight to get away from me as she watched me wide-eyed. I tucked the torn panties into my back pocket before kissing my way down her body as my fingers worked her clit.

"Be a good girl for me, Angel, and I'll let you come." I whispered against her breast as I took her nipple into my mouth through her shirt.

"Fuck you," she moaned, using her hips to wiggle her way from underneath me.

I bit her nipple harder, forcing a pained noise to escape her throat. "Play nice."

I wanted both her pain and pleasure. I planned to take her whether she wanted it or not at that moment. Her powerless fight did nothing but make me harder for her. I licked down her exposed stomach, delighting in the shivers my tongue invoked. She continued to worm her way out of my grip as my mouth reached its destination between her soft thighs. I wasted no time devouring her, moving my hands to pin her legs open. Her sweet taste exploded on my tongue and I ate her like a starved man. She slipped her hand into my hair, pulling on the lengths hard as my name slipped from her full lips. I'm not sure if she intended to pull me off or force me to stay, but it would take more than her to stop me from feasting on her. I bit and sucked until she was grinding her pussy against my face, mewling like the little demon she was as I took from her. If I was ever to die, I wanted her cunt to be my last meal on this earth. Slipping my fingers into her and focusing my mouth on her swollen clit, I worked her into a frenzy. Oh, so quickly her walls clamped around my fingers as her orgasm overtook her. Her screams of pleasure filled the room as I feasted on her. Before she could come down, I unbuttoned my slacks, freeing my rock-hard cock. I quickly slipped up her body and slammed into her, as her pussy gripped my length. A moan slipped from my lips at just the feeling of her warm heat wrapped around my shaft. She tried to claw at my face to fight me off, so I pinned her hands above her head as I pistoned into her hard and fast.

"Get the fuck off me," she screamed, bucking her hips, which only forced me deeper inside of her wet center.

I grinned, leaning my face down to hers, "Now, why would I do that when you're taking me so well, Angel?"

Before she could scream at me, I captured her mouth with mine in a hungry and angry kiss. There was nothing nice about it with her teeth biting my lip until I could taste blood. The metallic taste sent me into a frenzy and I wanted to make her bleed just as badly. I fucked her harder as I slipped my knife from my pocket with my free hand. The blade traveled up her thigh as I slowed my thrusts. At the feeling of the blade, she stopped fighting me and I leaned up to watch her as I slipped the blade to the inside of her thigh next to where I was fucking her.

"I asked you to play nice, Angel."

My response was simply a glare as I smiled down at her. She was at my mercy and she knew it. I stalled my thrust as I dug the tip of my blade into her skin. The blood seeped from the minor wound in the most beautiful shade of red. A hiss left her lips as I continued to slice a D into her delicate flesh. Once I was satisfied, I slipped out of her, released her hands, and leaned down to lick away the blood. I groaned at the metallic flavor mixed in with her unique taste. She had become my new favorite dessert.

"You will always belong to me, Angel." I glanced up at her to see her reaction. If looks could kill, I'd be a dead man.

"I belong to no man." She spat, though the fight seemed to have completely left her.

"Keep telling yourself that, baby girl." I sat back on the couch and pulled her so that she was on top of me, forcing her hands behind her back. Quickly sheathing myself back into her wet cunt, and thrust my hips up. I wanted to break her. I wanted to have her begging for my cock, but I enjoyed every moment of her fight until she was coming on my dick.

CHAPTER NINE

Angel

The first to arrive, only a few minutes after Damon had released me, was Dimitri who shot a glare at his brother, after he had caught me trying to get myself together and Damon tucking himself back into his slacks. I felt my face heat as he eyed us both.

"I see you two are getting to know each other better." He sighed, going over and pouring himself a glass of scotch.

Damon simply chuckled deeply as he took a swing from his tumbler, eyeing me over the rim of the glass. He was so openly proud of himself while I was trying to get over the confusion. My body wasn't getting the memo that I wasn't interested, much like Damon didn't know how to take no for an answer. Yet, the feeling of his come leaking down the inside of my thighs and the burn where he'd cut me had me wanting to do it all over again.

I went over and finished stocking the small private bar, making sure that I had everything I would need for the evening. I had every intention of pretending like Damon didn't exist and that what happened was a one-time thing. It was simply to get it out of my system so I could focus on my mission. He wanted to own me and he was shit out of luck if he thought he ever had a chance.

A group of businessmen in three-piece suits arrived shortly after Dimitri, followed by the one and only Madax. He entered the room and my blood ran cold. I felt suffocated, like his presence sucked up every bit of air in this small room. I forced myself to take a deep breath, plastered a sweet smile on my face as I greeted each man entering the room, and took their orders for the evening.

As I made everyone's drinks I watched Madax from the corner of my eye. He was fairly attractive for a man in his early sixties. He had short cut salt and pepper hair that he wore slicked back and a well-groomed matching beard. His chocolate eyes watched me closely as he spoke with the other businessmen. I could tell he was muscular and toned underneath his suit with just a hint of tattoos peeking out here and there. It was obvious where Damon and Dimitri got their tall, built frames. They each carried a sense of confidence about themselves and took pride in their appearance.

Dimitri was the most businesslike and conservative of the three. He had the same light brown hair as Damon, but was clean-shaven, had no noticeable tattoos, and carried himself like I would imagine a politician. He was calm and collected, watching everything going on with poise, and if you weren't paying enough attention, you'd miss the tick in his jaw and flex of his fingers around his glass every time someone said something he didn't like.

Madax carried himself in the same fashion as Dimitri and was presented as a businessman. The only difference was that the tattoos gave him a slightly rough around the edges look. That he could play the part of a gentleman, but he's also put a bullet in your head if you crossed him.

Damon was the most brutal of the bunch. You could tell he took pride in his appearance like the other two, but he was laid back in his dress and demeanor. He was the kinda bad boy the ladies would trip over to get just a second of his time. His smirk that lifted just noticeably higher on the left side, and the excited twinkle in his eye made him dangerous. He was a wolf in sheep's clothing that would take pleasure in killing a man.

These men were each dangerous in their own way.

Loading my tray up with the drinks and making my way around the room, saving Madax for last. I smiled at him while he watched me like a predator who had just spotted its next kill. I leaned down to hand him his glass, and he quickly placed his hand on my thigh.

"You're the new girl, darling?" He drawled in his seductive tenor. I bet that worked on all the young girls. All I wanted to do was break the fingers that were trailing lightly up my leg.

I decided playing shy would be the best route to go, so I forced myself to blush. "Yes, sir."

I was a perfect fucking actress. I'd been playing this role for the past eight years and the men I set my sights on always ate out of the palm of my hands.

He smirked as he slid his hand to the back of my knee and pulled me closer. "Why don't you sit next to me for now and relax? We are all good with drinks for the time being."

It wasn't a request, and I knew it. Stealing a glance at Damon, who was watching the exchange from across the coffee table. Anger filled his eyes and his grip on the tumbler in his hand had tightened enough to leave him white-knuckled. I sat next to Madax while his hand rested just above my knee as he went back to talking business with the other men. I didn't care to learn their names or even understand most of what they spoke of. Cattle, stock, livestock, and market were mentioned, but from the sounds of things, I had the sinking feeling they weren't talking about farm animals. I sat perfectly still, unable to fully relax while watching the interactions between them. As the night drew on, Madax's hand would work its way up my thigh and he'd try to include me in the conversations. While I wasn't comfortable, Madax was as gentlemanly as a snake of his kind could be. I guess that was part of the allure. He may be the gentleman on the outside, but I knew he was far from a good man. My sister's dead body proved that.

"Angel, would you mind grabbing me another?" Damon asked, shaking his empty glass. I nearly jumped at the opportunity.

"Of course, sir," I said as I made my way over to retrieve his empty glass. He grabbed my wrist lightly as he whispered so that only I could hear.

"You're doing great. Just try not to kill him yet." He smirked.

I shot him a glare, "I'm aware," I growled under my breath as I took his glass and went to get him and the others a refill.

Thankfully, Madax didn't pay me much mind while he finished conducting business. I went about cleaning up from the evening and doing an inventory of everything that would need to be restocked for the private bar.

I didn't turn around to face the men as they each filed out of the room, so it came as a surprise when a hand rested on my lower back and the smell of gin fanned across the side of my face.

"Thank you for the service tonight, darling." Madax breathed across my neck. His hand skating lower on my ass. Not enough to make him out as a complete pervert, but enough to get the message that he was interested.

"It was my pleasure, sir."

He placed a gentle kiss on my cheek, slipped a crisp $100 bill on my tray, and walked towards the door. I stood there with my hands clenched at my sides until I heard the click of the door shutting. Without thinking, I grabbed a tumbler and hurled it at the wall, watching as it shattered. He'd been right fucking there, with his hands on me most of the night, and I'd had to play nice instead of killing him and all those posh business men.

Damon chuckled behind me, and I glared at him over my shoulder. "What's so fucking funny?"

He walked over to me, lightly running his finger tips up my arm, "The fact that you're such a good little actress. You nearly had me convinced with the shy, innocent act," he slid his fingers up my shoulder before wrapping his hand around my neck, forcing me onto my tiptoes to be in his face, "I know much better than that, Angel."

He caged me up to the bar top as he spoke lightly, running his fingers along my arms as he placed gentle kisses along my neck.

"What happened tonight won't be happening again." I shrugged him off to go clean up the glass all over the floor.

"Keep telling yourself that, Angel." He walked out without glancing my way, leaving me to clean up my mess.

CHAPTER TEN

Angel

The rest of the weekend and the beginning of the week went as normal following the meeting with Madax. He hadn't shown up again at the club after his business partners left Saturday night. After the meeting, I had to rush home and scrub my skin to the point of pain before I felt clean. That was the biggest downfall of doing crap like this. I felt dirty until I could wash that grim away with the blood of the men who'd hurt Jessica.

It was Thursday afternoon at the club when I received any contact from Madax. I received a delivery, which included a diamond Tiffany necklace and a note saying, *I haven't been able to stop thinking about you.* What was the deal with the Ashford men thinking they could just touch me and send me gifts afterward, like it was completely normal? The thought alone made me roll my eyes and toss the jewelry box into the cabinet that housed my belongings during work hours.

Things had been weird between Damon and me since our short fling. He'd kept his distance, only lightly brushing me in passing, and I would constantly feel his eyes on me whenever he was at Hellfire during my shifts. I wasn't sure about my feelings anymore and the on-and-off-again thing was really pissing me off, no matter how hard I tried to ignore the entire situation. I finished my shift and headed straight home to collapse on my bed. The events of the past week had exhausted my system, but I needed to get my shit together. I could worry about all that tomorrow.

I awoke to a knock on my door and pulled my blankets high above my head. It was far too early for people to be knocking on my door on a Friday morning. My head was pounding, and I felt like I hadn't slept nearly enough. After waiting a good 15 minutes, I got up to see what those Ashfords had sent this time.

Opening the door, there was a decently sized white box tied with a cream-colored silk ribbon. Picking it up, I closed the door and fished out the little card.

Be ready in this by 5pm. I will have a car sent to pick you up. Don't worry about work, I have cleared it with your boss. -Madax

Opening the box, I found a white dress and a matching lace mask. Glancing at the clock, it was almost three in the afternoon. I'd slept longer than I had realized, yet was still feeling run down. Since it was going to be a formal event, I might as well get ready. I bathed, taking extra care of my beauty routine, before getting dressed. Slipping into the dress, it fell to the floor to pool out around my feet. It was a floor-length white gown with slits up both sides to my hips, with a tulle-covered skirt that did little to cover up the exposed skin. It had spaghetti straps and a deep plunging neckline that fell to my navel. I took time to apply light, natural makeup with my usual bold red lip. Something about the color gave me a sense of power and control when dealing with the men I'd been hunting. I threw my hair up in a messy yet elegant, low bun, leaving stray pieces to frame my face in natural waves. To finish the look, I slipped on a pair of gold gladiator heels and the white lace masquerade mask. Looking at myself in the mirror, I barely recognized myself. I looked elegant and sophisticated. Worst of all, the white color of this dress made me sick. Why couldn't it have been something darker?

At exactly 5pm there was a knock on the door and I took one more chance to make sure everything was perfect. I opened the door to see who my escort would be for the evening. My breath caught in my throat seeing Damon standing there in an all-black tux, shiny black loafers, and his long hair tied up into a sleek high bun. He'd taken the time to groom his roguish beard, and I had the sudden urge to touch it. It had surprised me at how soft it felt when he went down on me Saturday night. His blue eyes traveled over my body like a heated caress, and I felt my face flush. He smirked in the charming, crooked way that only he could when his eyes met mine again and he stepped to the side, offering me his arm.

Glaring at him, I slipped my arm into his as he escorted me out of the building. We definitely didn't seem to fit into my crappy apartment building dressed like this. I'd never felt so out of place here. Damon didn't seem to pay it any mind as he led me out front to an elegant black limo. He opened the door, allowing me to slide in before he took a seat next to me.

"I wasn't expecting you to pick me up when I got the letter from Madax." I glanced anywhere but at him.

He slid his hand up my neck before forcing me to look at him. "I wouldn't miss a chance to have you to myself."

His voice was deep as he gripped my chin, pulling me closer to him. His free hand inched up my exposed thigh until he reached my center, a groan leaving his lips when he noticed that there was nothing underneath my dress.

"Angel," He growled, claiming my lips with his.

The kiss was hungry and forceful. I kissed him back just as furiously. My hands gripped the front of his jacket as I worked the buttons loose in a frenzy to get to him. He pushed me back onto the seat while he sat between my legs, lifting the skirt of my dress up, baring my aching center to him and his mercy. So much for not letting this happen again.

He leaned down to trail kisses up my thighs as he reached behind him, pulling a hidden handgun out, which he laid on the seat next to him. At the sight of it, I gasped, sitting up and sliding away from him. My retreat must have been amusing, because he just smirked at me, a dark chuckle leaving him as his hand wrapped around my ankle to keep me from moving too far.

"Don't worry, baby girl. That isn't for hurting you." He cornered me, pinning me to the side of the limo by my throat, and slid his finger up my inner thigh.

He took his time exploring the valleys between my thighs with his free hand, sending goosebumps down my legs. His sinful mouth trailed kisses along my chest and the hand around my throat moved to release my cleavage from the dress. He took my peaked nipple into his mouth, biting down on the tinder flesh to the point of pain. It was a direct line to my wet center, and I tried to grind my hip to get any sort of friction where I needed it. He chuckled, causing his beard to tickle me where I was most sensitive, and he moved his teasing hand to my swollen clit.

"Is this what you want, Angel?" He asked before taking my other nipple into his mouth.

"Fuck… yes." I moaned out breathlessly.

This man knew exactly what he was doing. He slipped two fingers into my pussy while his thumb worked my clit. My nails dug into his shoulders as I rode his hand, seeking the pleasure my body craved. He moved down my body in a fluid motion until he was between my legs, moving his hand to take my clit into his mouth. Sucking and biting to give me the perfect mix of pain and pleasure. I'd never thought of myself as a masochist, but every time he hurt me, it turned me on.

As he worked me with his fingers and expert tongue, I watched as he reached for the gun he'd taken out earlier. The cold metal of the gun trailed my thigh to my wet center, sending shivers in its wake. Damon forced my legs wider, replacing his fingers with the gun, as he ran his tongue along my slit. The sensation of his rough beard, his warm tongue, and the cold of the gun sliding along my center had me panting. I felt him smile against my skin as he slowly pushed the barrel into me, forcing a breathy moan to escape my lips.

"You're taking it so well, Angel. Has anyone ever made you come like this?" He asked, lifting his head to look at me. I couldn't seem to form words as I shook my head. He began thrusting the gun into me at a hard yet leisurely pace. The cold and unusual feeling forced me to moan in pleasure. He had the gun angled just right to stimulate that sweet spot within me, and his hand rubbed my clit for the perfect amount of friction.

"That's it, baby girl. I want to watch you come on my gun." He purred as he thrust it harder and faster. My pussy clenched tightly around the barrel as he brought me closer to my release.

Damon lowered his mouth back between my legs and I felt as he licked the healing mark where he'd brand me. How could the fact that he'd marked me in such a way make me feel cherished and so fucking turned on at the same time? I rocked my hips, moaning out his name softly.

"Fuck… Damon… please don't stop."

"I love it when you beg." He groaned before moving his mouth to my center, taking my clit into his mouth, sucking and biting at it in the perfect rhythm to match the thrusts of his gun.

I gripped his hair tightly as I rode his mouth and gun. All I could focus on was the pleasure he was bringing me as I screamed out my release. The feeling of my pussy clenching around the gun's barrel had me tipping over the edge harder than I ever had. He devoured me like his favorite meal through the waves of pleasure until I was gasping to catch my breath.

He removed the gun from between my legs, lifting it to my lips. "Clean up your mess, baby girl."

I wrapped my lips around the barrel, moaning at the flavor of myself mixed with the metallic taste of the gun. I never took my eyes off his as I cleaned my release from his gun, removing it from my mouth with an audible pop.

He slipped the gun back into its holster on the waistband of his pants and helped me into a seated position, pulling me closer to his side, and peppered light kisses along my neck, whispering praises.

"Such a good girl, Angel." He placed one more rough kiss against my lips before pulling my dress back into place to cover me. "We will be there in just a moment."

I was still completely at a loss for words. I wasn't sure why I let him touch me when I'd already said it wouldn't happen again. Lost in thought, I glanced out the window and watched as we pulled through the iron gates of a large estate. The driveway was paved and lined with beautiful trees that were changing colors in the growing autumn atmosphere. It led up to a large white colonial estate that screamed money. Everything was lit up and appeared to glow in the dusk that was descending over the horizon. In another life, I may have found it beautiful, but I had learned that most beautiful things were a mask meant to hide someone's dirty secrets.

As we pulled to a stop, I watched as others dressed in flowing gowns and tuxedos made their way through the elegant double-doors of the estate. The women appeared to be the only ones wearing masks for this event. Damon climbed out first, offering me his hand as he helped me to stand. I made sure that my dress was in place after our little adventure on the way here, before Damon led me up the front steps. Everything with the house was almost comical, with its white and gold accents, oversized double doors, white marbled floors, expensive artwork, crystal chandeliers, and the grand double staircase that was the centerpiece as you entered the foyer.

Damon led us to an extravagant, golden ballroom that was filled with people for whatever this occasion was. I took in every exit I could use if needed and watched as servers offered champagne and hors d'oeuvres to the guests. We made our way to the back corner of the room where I could see Madax surrounded by a group that was hanging on to his every word, as he spoke of how his family came into power and made their first billion. I scoffed under my breath, which just made Damon smile.

"Play nice tonight, Angel." He said, patting my hand lightly.

As we neared, Madax's eyes snagged on me. Eyeing me like the predator he was as he took in every inch of my exposed skin. I felt my hand tighten on Damon's arm and he squeezed it in reassurance before presenting me to Madax.

"Sir," He said, moving my hand from his arm to place it into his father's.

"Thank you for escorting this lovely woman for me this evening, son." Madax pulled me close to him, wrapping an arm around my waist and resting his hand far too low on my hips for me to be comfortable. I simply smiled up at him. These Ashford men had a way of making a girl feel small with their 6 feet plus of stature. I wasn't short, standing at 5'5", but they made me feel small. Damon was slightly taller than his father by a few inches, as he stood off to the other side of Madax, speaking to an elderly man in the group.

Pressed into his side, Madax went on with his previous conversation while I pretended to hang onto his every word, like the others in our small circle. Glancing away from Madax, I noticed that Damon had slipped away. I could just barely see him standing at the bar along the wall closest to our little group through the growing crowd.

He kept watch like this throughout the night as Madax paraded us around the room and light instrumentals played. It became clear quickly that I was to be seen and not heard. So I played the part of the dutiful mistress, who smiled and nodded when appropriate. Only speaking when directly spoken to, as I noticed the other women doing. As I walked around the room, I also noticed the sheer lack of women. What was the point of so few women and why were we the only ones wearing masks?

I watched as Madax waved Damon back over towards us and he said goodbye to the group he was finishing up speaking to. When Damon got closer, he offered me his arm, and I was thankful as Madax let me go to him.

"Damon, keep Angel company while I finish business for the evening," He ordered before turning his attention to me, "Darling, please stay close to my son for the rest of the evening. I promise you will have my full attention once I'm finished with tonight's event."

I smiled at him as he kissed my hand lightly before making his way through the crowd to the large stage set off to the far side of the room. Damon placed his hand on the small of my back as he led me as far from the stage as he could. Dimitri was standing next to the door that led back out to the front of the house, and I waved slightly as he cut a glare in my direction. Him not liking me brought a smile to my face. He was right not to trust me. I'd proven that I was a wildcard in their plan, but we needed each other's help.

We stood against the wall together, with me between the two Ashford brothers, as the room fell into darkness and a spotlight shone towards the stage where Madax stood behind a white podium. It was obvious he really liked the color white.

Damon leaned down, placing his lips against the shell of my ear, forcing a shiver to work down my spine. "This next part of the night you aren't going to like."

I glanced up at him to meet his eyes as he straightened, tilting his head towards the stage and pulled me in closer to his side. The room had fallen silent as Madax became the center of attention.

"Thank you, everyone, for joining me this evening. We have a large stock tonight and I'm sure you will all be very pleased. Tonight's stock is full of fresh, untouched products," Madax smiled at the crowd as a line of women were brought onto the stage. They were each in chains and dressed in all colors of lingerie.

The crowd cheered and clapped while I just stood there frozen. My breath caught in my throat as I gaped at the stage. I was sure my face looked like those old cartoons where their jaws hit the floor. I had been expecting bad things from Madax, but this was an auction for women and girls to be sold off like property. Every muscle in my body tensed and I saw red as the first girl, probably no older than 16, was auctioned off to the highest bidder. I couldn't tear my eyes from each girl with tear-streaked faces being sold off like cattle. Never had I felt a blood lust so apparent that I could taste it. I had wanted him dead before. Now I wanted to watch him bleed out in front of me. I want to hurt him, not only for my sister, but for every girl that has ever stood on that stage.

What sort of sick fuck could do this to other people? I went to pull away from Damon, but he just held me tighter, pinning me to his side as he watched the scene play out in front of us. Glancing at his face, I could see the same anger in his eyes that I was feeling. He wasn't on board with this bullshit which made me like him more.

"We don't like this any more than you do." I heard Dimitri's gruff voice on my other side.

"He's a dead man walking," Damon growled as he ground his teeth.

Glancing around, we were the only three in this room that didn't like what we were seeing. I silently wondered if the other women here were upset by what was going on or if they just simply supported it. They just stood there and partook in this shit and I wanted to hurt them, too. How could they just stand there and allow it?

We simply stood there in silent, boiling anger as each girl was sold and escorted away to be claimed at the end of the night. I don't know how I simply stood and watched. Every fiber of my being was begging to be let loose on this crowd of monsters. I might not be a saint, but I wasn't downright evil. Not like this. Damon's arm stayed locked around my waist, holding me in place as the night went on. Twenty-three girls were sold that night, ranging from the age of 16 to 25.

As they sold the last girl, a toast was made, and the crowd filled out. Either to leave for the evening or to collect their prize. Dimitri slipped off and Damon led me upstairs away from the people, into what he said was a guest room I'd be using during my stay here.

By this point, I was in a daze as I sank down onto the edge of the bed and simply stared at the bare, white walls of the room. Damon crouched down in front of me, taking my hands in his and placed soft kisses along my knuckles.

"This is part of the reason that we wanted your help. He expects Dimitri and I to try something. You're the only one who can get close to him without raising suspension." He whispered.

I let my eyes roam over his face, looking for any sign that he was lying, only to find none. All I could see was his godly beauty, like some viking warrior kneeling at my feet. I never would have thought I'd find a man as rugged as him, beautiful, but he was. He was a good man who liked to do bad things, and it drew me to him like a moth to a flame. His full lips, soft beard, deep blue eyes that could do in any woman, and in that moment I wanted him. I wanted him to make me forget what I had just witnessed. Without a second thought, I crushed my lips to his, pulling him closer toward me by the collar of his jacket, forcing him in between my legs as I begged him with my mouth to make everything else disappear. Just for a moment. Fuck what I had said. I wasn't sure there would ever be a last time with this man.

He kissed me back, slipping his hand into my hair to angel me just how he wanted me as he ravished me. His tongue demanded entry as he tasted all of me, with a hunger I could only describe as pure Damon. We stayed like that, gripping onto each other, our hands roaming, until someone cleared their throat at the door.

We both startled apart and glanced towards the door, where Madax stood with a glare towards his son. His tuxedo jacket was unbuttoned and his tie undone as he walked into the room running a hand through his slicked back hair. His eyes traveled between me and Madax. I wasn't sure what he saw on my face, but whatever he saw made him smile wickedly.

"I see you two get along fairly well." He said as he slipped off his jacket and tossed it on the bed, rolling up the sleeves of his white dress shirt.

"Let's see just how well." He said as he slid a glare back towards Damon.

CHAPTER ELEVEN

Damon

I simply stood there and watched as my father looked at the two of us. I hadn't meant for us to get caught, and I wasn't sure what the twisted fuck had in mind. Whatever it was, I knew for a fact it was going to piss me off and go too far with Angel. Angel simply watched every move he made with a mix of hate and confusion gleaming in her eyes. Just waiting to see what the old fuck would do next. The smile he was wearing made it obvious he didn't see what I saw on her face.

"Stand up darling, and undress for me." My father instructed her.

She glanced towards me, which only made my father's smile widen. "Oh, he gets to watch, darling."

She looked back at him and stood, slipping the dress off her shoulders for it to pull at her feet, leaving her in nothing but the golden heels she'd worn tonight. Just seeing her bare was making me grow hard and tented my pants. I took a glance at my father to see him adjusting himself as he prowled towards her, running his fingers lightly over her stomach and breast. He whispered praises as he explored her body, slipping his fingers between her legs as he stood behind her, plunging them into her with no warning. He wanted me to watch as he touched her and was making sure I could see everything he did. She simply stood there with a blank look on her beautiful face and her jaw tensed. He continued to finger her as he forced her to lean over the bed with her ass in the air and he continued to work the cunt that belonged to me. Throughout it all, she stayed quiet, breathing through her nose, her body tense. She didn't make the same noises for him as she did for me. That only filled me with pride. I would be the only man to make her feel like that again. I intended to keep my Angel.

It took everything in me to stand there and watch when he unbuttoned his pants to free his lack-luster dick and lined it up with her cunt. The only sound that left her as he thrust into her was a pained gasp and she fisted the sheets, turning her face to look at me as he pounded into her from behind. I couldn't take my eyes off hers. Watching the pain and hatred wash over her features. From the sounds of it, she wasn't wet for him at all as he pounded away at what was mine. No deliciously wet sounds of skin meeting skin that filled the space when I was balls deep in her glorious pussy. The old fuck didn't care if she wanted it or not. He simply demanded it.

"Get on the bed and fuck this whore's face," my father grunted as he continued to fuck her.

I kept watching Angel's face as I made my way over to the bed and climbed in front of her. I undid my pants, freeing my cock as I pulled her up to take me into her mouth. God, her mouth felt so good as I slid between her wet lips. Those blood-red lips wrapped beautifully around my cock. I wanted to fuck up her pretty makeup and have it smeared across her face. The anger in her eyes quickly morphed into hunger as I fucked her mouth roughly, forcing myself deep into her throat. She moaned around my cock, sucking on me. The old fuck might have thought the sounds were for him, but I knew her pleasure was only for me. I wanted this to end for her quickly, but I also wanted to enjoy the filling of her mouth around my straining cock. So, I fucked her mouth just like I would her cunt. Hard and deep. Forcing her to gag on my size as I chased my release. Her saliva dripped down my balls as she took me like a good little slut. Tears ran down her face, leaving blackened streaks down her cheeks. Thank god she could take my size. Few women could.

My father groaned as he pulled out of her, coming over her cunt and ass. He was a fucking idiot if he thought she was his. I stilled my hips without getting my release, pulling out of her mouth to give her some relief. She stayed there panting to catch her breath and cast her eyes down to the now wrinkled duvet.

"Clean her up," my father ordered as he picked up his jacket and left the room without so much as a word towards Angel.

Once he was gone, I quickly cleaned up his mess with my shirt before pulling Angel up into my arms on the bed and forced her onto her back as I crushed my lips to hers. I wanted to brand myself on her. Force every touch my father had inflicted away so that she only remembered mine. That it was only me who her body would sing for. She kissed me back, clawing at me like a feral feline as her figures tore through my skin. I forced myself between her thighs and slammed my cock deep inside of her wet, warm cunt. Her back arching off the bed from the force as I fucked her hard, just like I knew she liked. Her hands slid around to my back, digging her nails into the skin as she gripped for purchase. I reached between us, finding her clit, rubbing her to create the friction she needed. Oh so quickly, she came apart underneath me with my name falling from her lips. I followed her just as quickly, burying myself deep inside of her as I filled her, her tight cunt milking me through both our releases.

CHAPTER TWELVE

Angel

I awoke surrounded by the scent of mahogany and sweet apples. Strong, tattooed arms held me around the waist with my back pressed against a hard chest. Damon had spent the night fucking me until I couldn't remember my name. I didn't even remember falling asleep next to him.

It had been a nice way to end my horrific evening. Between the auction and the feeling of Madax inside of me, I needed a moment to forget. Damon was a wonderful distraction that I was becoming more and more addicted to. The manly scent of him alone had heat pooling in the pit of my stomach and I rubbed my thighs together, moaning at the slight pain it caused. Every ache was caused by Damon's massive cock, and I loved every second of it.

Damon's arm tightened around me, pulling me closer to him as I felt him grind his hard cock between my legs. It rubbed just right against my clit every time, forcing breathy moans to leave my lips. He was already slick from me as he continued to slide along my slit.

"Is this for me, Angel?" He asked. His voice sounded deeper and scratchier with sleep as he woke.

I didn't answer him, instead choosing to enjoy the feeling of him teasing me in the most perfect way. Without any warning, he angled his hips and slammed deep inside of me. He fucked me mercilessly and spent the rest of the morning making me beg for release. It was the sweetest of tortures as he toyed with me, but refused to let me come.

"Don't you dare come, baby girl." He rammed into me with each word.

I was so fucking close and every time he'd get me to that edge he'd order me not to come, "Fuck, please."

I was to the point of begging. Wanting to chase my release, and nearly screamed when his thrusts slowed. I didn't like this game. I didn't like begging him. I'd never begged for anything from a man, and he had accomplished it with hardly any effort.

His thrusts were slow and deliberate as he fucked me from behind, pinning my hands behind my back with only one hand. His other hand smacked my ass as I tried to push my way back to get the friction I'd need to come. "Bad girls don't get to come, Angel."

He slammed into me one last time, sheathing himself to the hilt and held himself there. His hand moved from my seared cheek and traced lightly to my ass, where he pressed his finger in just enough to let me know he was there. A gasp left my lips, and he pushed his finger in just a little deeper. I was so turned on he didn't even need lube.

"Has anyone ever touched you here, Angel?" He asked as he fucked my ass with his finger.

Words failed me and I shook my head, whimpering at the pain and stretch as he added a second finger.

"So tight for me, Angel. I want this ass to be mine, and only mine." He pulled out of me as he continued to fuck my ass and released my hands.

I gripped the sheets as the pain morphed into an aching pleasure. Thrusting my hips back into his hand, moaning softly into the blankets. I could hear the slick sound of him fisting his cock, which just spurred me on. It didn't take me long to realize he'd lubed up his cock. He removed his fingers and positioned himself at my ass, pushing just enough to break through that barrier of muscles as he slowly slid inside of me.

"Fuck, Angel," he groaned once he was completely inside, holding himself there for me to adjust.

He reached around to my clit, working the bundle of nerves until I was moaning and thrusting my hips back, causing a moan to fall from his lips.

"Such a good little fucking slut for me, Angel." He praised as he thrust into my ass, his fingers never leaving my clit.

He worked me until I was about to explode, his hips faltering slightly as he reached his own release, "Come for me, baby girl," He groaned out as he slammed into me one last time.

It was the only thing I needed to topple over that edge of pleasure, screaming his name into the sheets as the hardest orgasm I'd ever had washed over me.

It was well after lunchtime when Damon finally left me. He had left a pair of his spandex boxers and a black band shirt that would swallow me in the attached bathroom so that I could shower and freshen up. Damon had taken it upon himself to go collect "some things" from my apartment. Making it clear I was staying here for a while longer.

I took my time in the shower and got some much needed time to myself, deciding to go find something to fill my empty stomach before Damon returned. We'd head to Hellfire for the night soon after he brought me my things. The house was exactly what you would think of when you thought of rich pricks with far too much money. All the white and gold had me wanting to break something. Just to add a bit of chaos to the pristine place.

I found my way into the kitchen and started putting together something to eat and a pot of coffee. After the long night I had, with very little sleep, I'd need more caffeine than usual to get through my shift tonight. I settled at the white marble-topped island with a steaming cup of coffee and a bowl of mixed fruits I'd found in the fridge.

I was enjoying my alone time until Madax made his appearance of the day. He slipped into the kitchen and made himself a cup of coffee before coming to sit beside me. When he sat down, he slipped his hand up my thigh, resting it at the hem of the boxers I had on.

"I take it you had an enjoyable evening, darling?" He asked, taking a sip from his mug.

I simply smiled before popping a grape into my mouth, "Of course, sir."

His hand trailed farther up my leg to my center, rubbing me through the thin material of the boxers. "I would hope so with all that noise you were making."

As if called by the devil himself, Damon walked into the kitchen at that moment, though Madax didn't stop his exploring hand. Glancing at Damon, I could see how intently he watched Madax's other hand as it slipped under my shirt to pinch and tease at my breast. I could feel my body tensing, and not at all in a good way. Madax took his time playing with me. His hand rubbed at my clit through the thin material of the boxers I was wearing and I had to grip onto the edge of the countertop to keep myself steady.

This had become a game for him and felt more like punishment for me and Damon.

He pinched and pulled my nipple as it peaked at the attention. Fucking traitorous body of mine liked the attention even though I hated the man touching me. I stared, wide eyed, at Damon standing in the entryway. Madax moved his hand to slip into the boxers, inserting two fingers into my pussy as he worked my clit with his thumb. Last night he had been sloppy, but today he was pulling out all the stops to make me come.

Fuck, Madax was going to make me finish while Damon was forced to watch. My nails dug into the counter as my pussy clenched around Madax's fingers and a mewling sound left my lips as I came. It was nothing compared to what Damon did to me, but it had still happened and shame washed over me. Madax removed his now glistening fingers from me and licked them. He groaned as he tasted me without taking his eyes off my face. I couldn't look at either of them.

Damon cleared his throat, which seemed to grab Madax's attention. "Sir, we have to get ready for our shift at Hellfire."

I watched as he continuously fisted his hands at his sides. While he sounded calm and collected, his body language was saying something completely different. Madax just smiled as he took my hand in his, kissing the knuckles and smiling at me, almost sweetly.

"I'd love to take you out sometime this week while you're staying here. I haven't had you to myself." It wasn't phrased like a question, but as a demand. I had a feeling he never gave people the opportunity to tell him no, not that he'd listen even if they did.

I smiled and hoped it didn't look like a grimace. "Of course. How long am I going to be staying here?"

I must have been convincing, because his eyes seemed to twinkle in the light streaming in from outside. "As long as you'd like. I have some meetings, but I will see you again soon."

He stood, placing a light kiss on my cheek before leaving the kitchen, patting Damon on the shoulder as he passed with the hand he'd just used to make me come. I finished my bowl of fruit and coffee, rinsing them off to place in the dishwasher, while also avoiding looking at Damon. He was still tense and I couldn't stand to look at him after what had happened. I hadn't meant to, didn't want what had just happened. It made me feel dirty and sick to my stomach. I was also well aware I wasn't just free to leave, despite Madax saying otherwise. This was going to be a shit show.

CHAPTER THIRTEEN

Angel

Things had been fairly quiet where Madax was concerned while I stayed at his estate. The weekend had been busy, and I hadn't seen Madax except in passing. In those moments, he took every opportunity to touch me, but he hadn't demanded sex. On the other hand, Damon and I spent every moment together between our long nights, working at Hellfire, and spending our days prior to work wrapped up in each other's arms around the house.

I began to actually enjoy my time with him and couldn't seem to get enough. It hadn't been my plan to spend so much time with him when I was supposed to be seducing Madax. Madax had turned it into a game where he liked to touch me in front of Damon. He was controlling and demanding, as if he was trying to rub it in Damon's face that I was his and he was the one in control. I knew it was only a matter of time before he completely demanded my time and attention. That he was going to take me from Damon and stake his claim.

Tuesday, I took extra care to get ready for my "date" with Madax in my guest room. It bothered me being here and not in a space of my own, but being in the same house as my target would make getting close that much easier. I decided on a thigh length, red, strapless body-con dress, paired with black strappy heels for a simple yet bold look. My black hair was down in long beach waves and I applied light makeup with my signature red lip that matched the dress perfectly. As I was finishing up, I heard a light knock on the door.

"It's open." I didn't ever turn to look as Damon entered the room while I finished hooking the strap of my heel.

"Are you ready for tonight?" He asked as he crouched down in front of where I was sitting on the edge of the bed to finish hooking the strap of my shoe.

I simply glared at him before standing up to retrieve my bag from the top of the dresser. Opening it up, I checked to make sure I had everything I might need: my phone, wallet, knife, and a small handgun, just in case. Damon walked up behind me then, running his tattooed knuckles over my exposed arms. Tracing the patterns and line work of my tattoos.

"I can't protect you tonight."

I scoffed, brushing his hand off of me as I turned to face him. "I don't need you to protect me, Damon. I'm perfectly capable of handling this on my own. You aren't my protector. You're just a good fuck while I do a job."

I had expected him to be hurt, or at least angry at my comment. He surprised me when he simply flashed me his crooked smirk. Within a blink, his hand was around my throat, pinning my back against the dresser. Fuck, he was fast for someone so big. He stepped closer, no longer leaving any space between our bodies as he towered over me. With his hand around my throat, he forced me to look up at him, tightening his grip slightly.

"When this is over, you're going to beg to stay with me, Angel." He said from deep in his chest. The sound was more growly than usual and it had shivers racking across my skin.

He was fucking wrong. When this was over, I would fucking disappear, just like I'd always planned. My revenge would be complete and I could move on with my life. I didn't need him. Yes, getting close to him had gotten me close to Madax, but I would have killed him, regardless.

I glared up at him as he held me captive in his arms and spit in his face, "In your dreams."

He wiped his face with his free hand, the smirk on his face turning from entertained to one that made my heart stop. It was the smile of someone who was unhinged and I'd just poked the beast. I hadn't seen this side of him yet. His grip around my neck tightened, cutting off my air supply as I dug my nails into his wrist, trying to break his hold. Nothing seemed to faze him and his grip didn't slack until there was another knock on my door before Madax walked in.

Madax's eyes traveled between us, and Damon removed his hands from me, backing up to a reasonable distance. There was a mischievous twinkle in Madax's eyes as he took in the scene.

"I do hope I wasn't interrupting." He smiled, tucking his hands into the pockets of his slacks.

Tonight he was in a pair of light gray slacks, a white button up dress shirt with the two top buttons undone and sleeves rolled up to show the ink that covered his arms. His black dress shoes were polished to the point that they seemed to absorb the light in the room and his hair was in its usual slicked back style. His salt and pepper bread trimmed into a very put together style with just the right amount of rugged sex appeal.

I smiled in his direction while running my hands lightly down my dress to smooth out any wrinkles. "Of course not. Are you ready to go?"

"Whenever you are, darling."

I walked over to him, linking my arm with his as he led me out of the room. I wasn't even going to give Damon the satisfaction of glancing back at him.

Dinner was at one of the nicest places I'd ever been in. One of those places where you couldn't get in without a reservation months in advance. I was glad I had opted for a nicer dress, because even in that I felt slightly under dressed. From the looks of things, it was a fancy French place, and the menu wasn't even in English.

Madax took the chance to order an expensive bottle of wine for the table and to order something for me. I was surprised to learn that he spoke perfect French and was less surprised to find that he was a silent owner of the establishment. He sat across from me at a small round table that was covered in a cream tablecloth with a golden candelabra centerpiece. White roses rested in a small glass vase and left a light, sweet scent that mingled well with the aroma of food and wine.

I didn't have to speak much, as Madax was content to tell me all about the place and himself. I simply smiled, sipping my wine, and making small noises to let him know I was listening. The food came and went, while we enjoyed each other's company and spoke mostly about him. I was happy to just sit and listen and wasn't interested in telling him anything personal. If he did ask, I gave short answers or outright lied. He couldn't find out who I really was, but I was good at pretending to be someone else. I'd used the lies often enough in my time of working through the list of names responsible for what happened to Jessica.

"I'd love to know more about you. Do you have family in the city?" Madax asked me before taking a sip from his wineglass.

"No family. I've been on my own for most of my life." I said, taking a bite of the grilled chicken and vegetables in front of me.

"Oh, that sounds like it could be lonely for such a young woman."

"Sometimes, but I'm not alone now, am I?" I smiled sweetly at him.

My answer seemed to please him as his eyes took in every move I made. "No, you are most definitely not alone, darling."

More small talk followed until we finished with our meals and the bottle of wine. We left, deciding to walk down the streets of downtown. The streets were lined with businesses, restaurants, small shops, and a bit of everything else in between.

Madax had told me all about his business adventures, how he got his start and built his company from the ground up, how he'd lost his wife during childbirth and all the other personal things that I already knew from my research prior to seeking him out. Overall, the evening had been surprisingly nice, and we headed back to his estate, where he kissed me goodnight at my door.

I slipped into my room and gasped when I found Damon lounging on my bed, reading a book. I slipped off my heels, leaning back against the door to do so as I watched him flip through the pages of his book.

"Did you have a nice night, Angel?" He asked without glancing at me.

"I'd appreciate it if you'd leave." I said, walking over to toss my bag on the dresser. Turning my back from him as I began taking off the little jewelry I'd worn for the evening, placing it next to my bag.

I listened closely as he placed his book on the bedside table and made his way over to me. When he was standing next to me, his hands moved to push my hair over my shoulder and unzip my dress. Slipping it off my body, to pool at my feet and leaving me in my simple black lace thong. He took the chance to kiss along my shoulder and neck before turning me to face him.

"You have to answer for earlier, baby girl." He said, dragging his fingertips down my chest lightly.

CHAPTER FOURTEEN

Damon

I had spent the day pissed off about how things had ended with Angel earlier. As soon as she spit in my face, I wanted to bend her over and take my aggression out on her. I wanted to make her bleed and toe the line of pain and pleasure. Wanted to watch her beg on her knees while I brought her to the edge of release, only to deny her. I wanted to punish her.

When she walked into the room, I knew exactly how I'd get payback for the way she'd acted. She thought she'd just be able to leave whenever she wanted, but she was wrong. I owned her, whether she was willing to admit that or not.

I loved the way her skin flushed as my hands traveled down her chest to cup her breasts, kneading and pinching just the way I knew she enjoyed, as a small moan slipped past her ruby red lips. I took the opportunity to quickly lift her into my arms as her legs wrap around my waist and I captured her lips. I wanted to ruin that perfectly placed lipstick and have it smeared across her made-up face.

I carried her quickly to the bed I had prepared while she'd been gone. I pinned her hands above her head once she was pressed underneath me and handcuffed them to the headboard. As soon as the cold metal was holding her in place, she snapped her pearly white teeth at me in anger. The look she gave me only made me harder, as I thought up all the ways I could break her.

"What the fuck is this shit, Damon?" she pulled on the cuffs, but couldn't get them to budge as I pinned her legs down with my own.

"Payback," was the only response I gave her as I removed myself from on top of her, sliding off the bed.

I had made sure I could still flip her while handcuffed to the bed. Grabbing her by her ankles, I flipped her over onto her stomach before securing her legs to the bed. Looking down at her, all I wanted to do was sink my cock into her tight, wet cunt. To ensure she knew she wasn't the one in charge here, no matter what she may have thought. She would show me respect and if she didn't, I would punish her. I'd enjoy inflicting pain on her delicate flesh and watching her bleed the most beautiful shade of red.

I began unbuckling my belt and, at the noise, I delighted in the way her body tensed as she tried to glance at me over her shoulder. Removing the belt ever so slowly from the loops, I watched her pull on her restraints uselessly, before walking over to the side of the bed to lightly trail my fingers through her midnight hair.

"You look so pretty tied down, Angel." I praised gripping a handful of hair and pulling her head back to look up at me, " but I don't intend this to be completely enjoyable for you."

The anger in her eyes spurred me on as she locked eyes with me. I loved the fire in her that wouldn't allow her to back down from a fight. She wasn't afraid of me, death, or anything else. I wasn't sure I'd ever get enough of her. She was a snake and her venom was already slowly eating away at me from the inside out. I was hers and I was determined to make her mine.

I released her hair and stood next to the bed, bringing the belt down on her plump little ass. As it made contact, a loud smack filled the room, but she didn't make a sound. She simply put her face in the pillows and clenched her fists as I brought the belt down four more times until her ass was a beautiful shade of red. Once I was done, I dropped the belt to the floor. Leaning onto the bed. I rubbed the welts that decorated her perfect ass and placed light kisses along the deep red marks. The only noise to come from her was a slight gasp as she tensed under my soft touches.

Leaning back up to place a light kiss on her shoulder, I whispered gruffly, "You will learn to respect me."

She scoffed glaring at me over her shoulder, "Keep telling yourself that, asshole."

The glare didn't have the desired effect, as the hunger was apparent on her face with her wide, blown eyes. I simply smirked and brought my hand down on her already tender ass. "Be a good girl, Angel, and I'll let you come."

She bit her bottom lip instead of giving a smart comeback, "Will you play nice, Angel?"

"Fuck you."

That was probably the best I would get from her. I unhooked her legs and flipped her back over before taking my place between her thighs. Biting and nipping at the tender flesh up to the D marked on her inner thigh. She had been the only woman I'd ever felt the need to brand and just the sight had me straining against my jeans painfully. I slipped her panties ever so slowly down her legs and admired how my light touch had her skin flushed and goosebumps rising over her skin. Angel's mouth might have said she didn't want me, but her body was a completely different story.

I descended on her glistening cunt, devouring her until she was panting and wrapping her creamy thighs around my head. Wrapping my arms around those thighs, I lifted her off the bed to get the perfect angle as I ate my fill of her sweet nectar. Fuck, she was the sweetest thing I'd ever tastes. I wanted more, but tonight wasn't about her pleasure. She'd been a bad girl and bad girls didn't deserve to come. I licked and bit at her swollen clit until she was moaning my name and her thighs clinched tighter around my head. My Angel was so easy to please and I plunged my tongue into her wet heat. The muscles gripping at my tongue as I tongue fucked her mercilessly, slipping my hand around her thigh to work her clit. Just as she was about to come, I quickly dropped her to the bed, smiling down at her as I licked my lips.

"You fucking bastard!" She screamed in frustration, pulling at the cuffs while I simply knelt between her legs, unleashing my strained cock from my jeans.

"Such a greedy little slut, Angel." I fisted my cock, pumping it quickly as she laid there watching.

The anger in her eyes only fueled my desire as I brought myself to release. My come coated her stomach and cunt and a feeling of possession washed over me. The entire time she cursed me, but her eyes never left my cock. She was nearly entranced as the ropes of my release coated her. Once I was finished, I took my fingers to scoop up the mess I'd made and slide it into her aching center. Her pussy clenching around my digits as I pumped them in and out of her in a slow, torturous rhythm. I wanted as much of my seed in her welcoming cunt as I could force into her. She threw her head back in ecstasy as I worked to get her back to the edge of pleasure. The urge to have her come apart on my hand was great, and it took everything in me to remain in control. At the first signs of her orgasm, I moved my fingers out of her, stood from the bed and righted myself.

"Are you fucking kidding me!"

Her screams of frustration only made me smile as I walked out of the room, leaving her covered in my come and chained to the bed. She wouldn't be finding her release tonight. Bad little sluts didn't deserve it.

The night had been interesting listening to Angel scream as she fought to get out of her restraints. Things had finally quieted down just before midnight and I knew this morning she was bound to be in a horrible mood. I took my time making her coffee just the way she liked it, with just a splash of vanilla cream, and a plate of eggs, bacon, and fresh fruit. I hoped feeding her would give her pause to out right murdering me.

I opened the door to see her exactly as I'd left her. My dick was hard just seeing her naked body strapped to the bed as she glared out the window at the streams of morning light filtering into the room. She didn't look at me as I placed the tray of food and coffee on the bedside table.

"If you'll play nice, I will uncuff you so that you can shower and eat something before we leave for work today."

She nodded her head and continued to not look at me. That was probably the best response I would get. I fished the key from my pocket and made quick work of uncuffing each of her wrists. A mix of guilt and pride slammed into my stomach as I caught sight of the raw, red marks the cuffs had left on her from her struggles. I wasn't stupid enough to touch her yet, so I backed up as soon as she was free and sat at the foot of the bed. She said nothing as she climbed out of the bed and headed to the attached bathroom, slamming the door behind her. She was going to be a pleasure being around today.

CHAPTER FIFTEEN

Angel

I couldn't believe he had left me handcuffed to the bed all night long. My arms were sore and stiff from being held above my head, and I was exhausted. I had no idea how hard it would be to rest while restrained in a bed like that. With everything feeling so sore, I took my time in the shower just letting the hot water soothe my aching muscles.

Once I was out of the shower, I wrapped myself in a white silk robe, wrapped my hair in a towel, and made my way back into the room. Thankfully, Damon wasn't anywhere in sight, so I plopped down on the bed and pulled the coffee and plate of food closer to me. I was surprised to find the coffee still hot after my long shower, but thought nothing of it as I downed the cup.

Once my belly was full, I felt even more exhausted than I had in the shower. There was plenty of time before I had to be ready for my shift to get a little extra rest. I placed my empty mug and plate on the bedside table and drifted off to sleep.

Things were fairly busy, considering it was a Wednesday night. Zack, Cherry, and I were running from place to place, trying to make sure everyone had what they needed. According to some I had spoken to, a business convention was in town. With this being one of the hottest clubs in the city, they decided to all come here. While I was still feeling tired, I wasn't complaining when an attractive businessman tipped me a couple hundred at the end of the night.

Closing time was just 30 minutes away, so I decided to rush some things to the back storage room. On my way there, I heard a muffled scream from one of the back hallways leading to the bathrooms. I sat the box of bottles I'd been carrying on the floor and pulled my knife from its holster as I made my way towards where I'd heard the scream.

Rounding the corner, I came face to face with a man, pinning Cherry to the wall with his hand, working frantically to get her pants down her hips. Tears were running down her face as she struggled in vain to get the man off her. I inched up behind the guy as Cherry watched me with wide eyes.

"I'd get my hands off her if I were you, asshole." I said with venom dripping from my words. My knife was held to his jugular, drawing just the slightest bit of blood.

"You fucking bitch," He growled while backing away from Cherry.

I walked with him, never removing the blade from his throat until I could put myself in the space between them. He simply glared at me as he put his unremarkable dick back into his pants. From the looks of the beer gut and wrinkles, I had to say he was in his mid-sixties, which just made me want to hurt him more.

"Get the fuck out of here before I decide the world would be better off without you in it." I seethed.

"She isn't fucking worth my time, anyway." He scoffed and walked back towards the main room.

As soon as he was out of sight, I turned around and took a crying Cherry into my arms. No one fucking deserved that shit, especially not this sweet woman I'd come to know while working here. I simply held her while she cried, shushing her while I ran my fingers through her tangled blonde hair until she calmed down.

"Thank you so much. I don't know what he would have done if you hadn't shown up." She sniffled while wiping her tear-stained face on the sleeve of her black t-shirt.

I grabbed her face gently, forcing her to look at me. "There's no reason to thank me. No one deserves something like that to happen to them. Are you gonna be alright?"

She nodded her head, hiccuping the last of her dying sobs.

"Do you have somewhere to stay tonight where you won't be alone? I'd hate for that fucker to get any ideas and try anything while you're leaving tonight?"

"Not really. Dimitri is away on a business trip until Monday. It would just be me at home. I don't want to force Zack to come stay with me. He'd be far too protective and ask too many questions." She said, looking up at me with wide, fearful eyes.

I nodded, taking her into my arms again. "That's okay. You can stay with me at my place until he gets back."

I took her into the bathroom to help her get cleaned up. Once she was feeling a bit more like herself, we made our way to the front and let Zack know what had happened. He became the protective brother Cherry had said he would be, but with some reassurance he was fine with her staying with me until Dimitri was back in town. I grabbed mine and Cherry's things from the bar cubby and we headed back to my place.

Once we were inside my apartment, I quickly grabbed her an oversized t-shirt to change into after a shower, got her set up on the bed, and made her a mug of chamomile tea to relax.

"I know it's not much, but I promise that you'll be safe here the next few days. We can go over to your place tomorrow to grab whatever you need for the next couple of days." I said, sitting next to her with a cup of tea for myself.

"Thank you, Angel. I don't know how I'll ever repay you." She said as she finished the last of her tea and crawled into the bed.

I smiled at her, taking her mug into the small kitchen. "Get some sleep."

I cut off the lights and made myself comfortable on the couch and laid awake to the light sound of Cherry breathing. It hadn't taken her any time at all to get to sleep. I just hoped she would be okay, considering what she'd been through tonight. She reminded me so much of Jessica with that bubbly personality and innocence. I found myself wanting to protect her like I'd been unable to do for my sister.

The next day, we both slept in until almost noon before getting up to head over to Cherry and Dimitri's place. Once we were in their penthouse apartment, she got to work packing her suitcase while I took a look around. My apartment alone could have fit in their kitchen. It shouldn't have been a surprise that they lived in a luxury penthouse. I'd seen the estate and knew the kind of man Dimitri was. She told me she felt safer at my place when I mentioned that we could just stay here if it made her more comfortable.

"So, what's the story between you and Dimitri?" I asked as I looked over some photos of them hung along the wall of their living room. They looked happy. Even Dimitri was smiling in some of them. They had traveled together, and it painted a perfect picture of happily ever after.

"Well, that's an interesting story. I sort of grew up with the guys, since Zack and Damon were best friends growing up. We all kinda lived in the same neighborhood until Madax got his hands on some money and they moved into that big ass house. You'd never know it, but they came from nothing, just like me and Zack. Anyway, I was the only girl, so of course I'd beg to tag along with them whenever they went off doing whatever it was teenage boys do when they have far too much time and money. I'd always had a crush on Dimitri, but being so much younger than him, he didn't pay me any mind. I went off to college for two years before I realized it wasn't for me and we met back up when I came back to town. We started chatting while he was at Hellfire for business and he eventually asked me out on a date and that was that." She spoke while wheeling her suitcase to set in next to the door.

"I'm not going to lie. I was really surprised by it when Zack first told me. From what I've seen of Dimitri, you are both complete opposites. You're so bubbly while he's so… serious." I honestly wasn't sure how to describe him. He was stoic and more robot-like than human from my few interactions with him.

Cherry let out an airy laugh that matched her personality perfectly, "He's definitely the serious type, but once you get to know him, he's nothing but a big teddy bear."

"I'll have to take your word for that."

We spent the day lounging around her place and chatting. In those few hours, I'd gotten to know her on such a deeper level than I had anyone else since I was a kid. It was nice to sit and just relax. To talk and do something normal when usually I was on my own or on a personal mission. It felt as if a weight had been lifted off my shoulders for a bit and I was just as grateful to have this moment with Cherry as she had been for my help the night before.

CHAPTER SIXTEEN

Angel

The rest of the week flew by with Cherry. We spent the days shopping, talking, and doing all the normal things friends did, all while working the same shifts for the rest of the week. Thankfully, that fucker who'd tried to force himself on her hadn't tried to make another appearance, and by Saturday night, Zack had stopped hovering like a worried mother hen. It probably helped that we were slammed, but I assured him I would keep an eye out for Cherry.

The night had been a busy one, the busiest Hellfire had had since I began working here, anyway. I was beat and just wanted to head home to my bed, or couch, since Cherry was still staying with me. I said goodbye to everyone and ensured that Cherry was okay to drive herself to my place once she was done. Zack promised to let me know as soon as she was safe in her car and on the way, so I'd know when to expect her. I made my way out of the front doors and headed down the street to where I had parked my car. Just as I was about to unlock the doors, I felt someone wrap their arms around me and a gloved hand covered my mouth to hide the sound of a scream.

My first instinct wasn't to scream. Instead, I went into defensive mode. I threw my elbow back, hitting the guy hard enough in the ribs to hear a crack in the dead air of the night. When I heard the man yell out in pain, I took the chance to sling my head back, hitting him square in the nose. He finally let go of me to clutch the bleeding appendage as I whipped around. Only I hadn't expected a second man to be standing there who had a gun aimed at my head.

"Shit, I think this bitch broke my rib." The first guy whined as he cradled both his face and side. They both were dressed in all black with ski masks to hide their faces.

My hand instinctively went to the handle of my knife on my thigh as I slid my eyes between the two. I could just make out a white van down the alley behind them and I fought the urge to roll my eyes at the irony. These fuckers were trying to kidnap me, and I wasn't down without a fight. The one with the gun was the guy I needed to take out first, as he was the most dangerous. I couldn't think about it long though and quickly unholstered my blade, launching it at the man with the gun. It hit its mark in his right shoulder, causing him to drop the gun. The other one sprang into action, making a grab for me, but he didn't make it far when the sound of a gun went off and he crumpled to the ground. I took the chance to glance quickly towards where the gun went off to see Damon standing in the shadows with his gun drawn and a cigarette lit in his mouth. I glanced back at the man I had stabbed who was screaming like a little bitch trying to get my blade out of his shoulder. Picking up his discarded gun, I walked over to it and pointed it at his head, much like he had done with me.

"Word of advice. Don't point a gun at someone unless you have the balls to pull the trigger." I said before doing just that.

The loud sound of the bullet leaving the chamber left a slight ringing in my ears as he fell to the sidewalk. A steady pool of blood leaking from his fresh head wound. I removed my knife from his shoulder with a sickening slinking sound before turning to face Damon.

"I fucking had it under control."

He just smirked around his cigarette before walking away into the shadow of the alley that led back into Hellfire. Rolling my eyes, I took the gun and knife to throw into my car and headed home. I'd let Damon figure out the cleanup. I was sick of his games at this point.

CHAPTER SEVENTEEN

Damon

I'd been keeping my distance from Angel since she had left the estate and hadn't come back. I had assumed it was because she was mad at me, but according to Zack, she had just been watching out for Cherry. There had been an incident with some asshole Wednesday night and Angel had taken up the role of looking out for her until my brother was back in town.

I had planned to give her more space until Dimitri was back in town in the next few days, but I couldn't help but to get involved when I watched her gracefully take down the two assholes who had tried to grab her. I knew she could handle it, but I couldn't just let her have all the fun.

She had been pissed about my interference, so I left her without saying a word while she fumed and left. I had other things to worry about now. Not only did I need to call a clean-up crew for the bodies of those two pricks, I also needed to call my father and set things straight about how he wasn't supposed to have his goons taking girls directly from the club. The old fuck was going to get what was coming to him sooner than he realized.

I sat down at my desk, throwing my feet up, and dialed the number for my favorite cleaning lady, setting the phone down on speaker while I went about sorting tonight's paperwork.

"Boy, haven't you learned how to clean up your own messes yet?" The shrill older woman spoke as she answered.

Her tone was that of an elderly grandmother lecturing her grandchildren for sticking their hands in the cookie jar before dinner, making me smile. "Now Rosa, you know I couldn't do a thing without your expertise."

"Damn, straight. Give me the details and I'll send the boys out to get things settled. It's a busy night though, so it's going to cost you extra this time."

"I'll double it. Thank you, Rosa."

I gave her the details and went back to finishing up the paperwork for the night. I'd handle things with my fucking father in the morning. Who knew where the fucker was at this time of night. I finished up at Hellfire for the evening and locked up. I was beyond ready to put this night to rest and collapse into my bed. The only thing that would have made it better was if I'd be sharing it with a dark-haired spitfire.

Slamming my fists down on the desk, I growled in anger at the old fuck in front of me, "I don't give a shit what you have to do. They are your men, now get them in line or I swear to fucking god I'll destroy every bastard who tries to fuck with my club."

He just sat there coolly, typing away on his computer and not paying any mind to my outburst. I wanted to put a bullet in his head, but I couldn't do it here in the office of his legitimate business, Ashford Enterprises. It was a multi-billion dollar tech company that specializes in security. I clenched my fists at my sides, digging my nails into my palm to the point of breaking skin. It was his blood I wanted on my hands the most. I needed to keep my cool, or I was going to lose it.

"I'll see what I can do." He said, dismissing me as if none of this was his problem. For fuck's sake, he didn't even care that it had been Angel they'd tried to grab.

I turned, stomping to the door, but before I could slam the door he spoke once more, words that fueled my anger and I needed to hold someone's life in my hands.

"Bring Angel back home. It's time she realized she belongs to me and can't just go off whenever she feels like it. Also, inform her that your little fling is over."

I slammed the door shut so that there would be something between us stopping me from ending his miserable existence. Someone was definitely going to die today because I needed the fucking release. It had been far too long since I'd been able to play with someone and hold their life in my hands while they begged for the torment to end.

CHAPTER EIGHTEEN

Angel

For some reason, I ended up being the first person at work today. Cherry had taken the night off to prepare for Dimitri's arrival back the next day. Walking into the club with no one else here had the place feeling overly empty and a feeling of loneliness washed over me. It was dead silent as I walked behind the bar to drop off my things and get to work cleaning. I knew Damon was probably here since the place was unlocked, but I wasn't interested in seeing him right now.

I was just about done with organizing the bar for the night when I heard a muffled scream coming from the back. It definitely sounded like a man had screamed and it had me curious about who else could be here. I was positive that the noise wasn't coming from Damon. I tossed my cleaning rag on the bar top and made my way to the back. Following the screams that got louder as I made my way down the dark halls. I came up to the door that led to the basement. Zack had informed me when I started no one was allowed down there except for management, but that was definitely where the screams were coming from. The door wasn't locked, so I simply made my way down the dark stairs, being careful not to miss a step, as I couldn't even see a foot in front of me. Once at the bottom, I could tell it was a large concrete space with a few doors at the far end. One of said doors was cracked, causing fluorescent light to spill out into the open space and the screams were almost deafening this close. That is until it became eerily quiet.

I inched myself closer as quietly as possible until I was standing right outside the door. Peaking in, I could see a solid white room, covered in plastic, and blood splattered along the walls and floor. With my heart racing, I pushed open the door to get a better view, praying to whatever god or goddess would listen that it didn't make a sound. My breath caught in my throat at the sight in front of me. Damon stood in all his glory, facing away from me. His long hair was tied up into a high bun on his head, shirtless, with all his tattoos on display, and a pair of tight black jeans slung low on his tapered waist, showing off the sexiest ass I'd ever seen on a man. There was blood coating his body and arms. The sight had heat pooling at my core as I inched into the room. It was as if there were an invisible string pulling me closer to him.

There was a naked man hanging from chains that were attached to the ceiling. He was covered in blood and there was a large pool of it at his feet, which barely hung off the ground. He had obviously been tortured and by the fact his chest wasn't moving, the fat fuck was already dead.

I must have made a sound, because Damon turned around quickly to face me. Shock registered on his face at seeing me standing behind him. I could see the blood thirst still in his eyes and he tracked his eyes down my body. The action of his eyes devouring me left me feeling flushed, and I knew that if he were to reach under my skirt, he'd find me wet and wanting.

I didn't take my eyes off his face as I stepped closer and drug my fingers down his bloodied chest, "Early day in the office, boss."

A primal growl left his lips as he quickly grabbed me, pinning me between him and the opposite wall.

"You aren't allowed down here, Angel." He said in his deep, gravely voice.

It sounded huskier at the moment as his hand wrapped around my throat, forcing me to look up at him as he towered over my small frame. The thought of him being able to break me made me smile as I dug my nails deeper into his chest, earning me the most delicious groan from him. He tightened his hand around my neck to the point I knew if I pushed him anymore, I wouldn't be able to breathe.

I let my eyes travel down his body, taking in the beautiful mix of ink and blood. I'd never been more turned on at the sight of a man in my life and I wanted to feel all of him in that moment. "What are you going to do to me, *sir?*"

The innocent question had him gripping me tighter, and he took my mouth hungrily. Everything about being with Damon was primal and animalistic. He consumed me in these moments, and I was powerless to stop him, didn't want to. I wanted every part of him and I wanted him to drag me down into the depravity with him. I'd never wanted anything more in my life. That realization alone was terrifying, so I pushed it into the back of my mind as he began ripping at my clothes. He pushed me up the wall, causing me to wrap my legs around his waist. He made quick work of our clothes and slammed into my aching center without remorse. His hips thrust hard and fast into me, causing screams of pleasure to leave my lips as he consumed me. I held on tightly, thrusting my hips to meet his, forcing his enormous cock to hit me in just the right place until we were both moaning out our release.

I thought maybe that would be the end of it, but he was still hard inside of me as he pulled me down to the floor with him. He had me on top as he forced me to ride him, using his firm hands on my hips.

"That's it, Angel. Use me for your own pleasure."

It was all the encouragement that I needed as I slid my soaking pussy up his dick before slamming back down repeatedly. The groans of pleasure he let loose spurring me on as I drove us both over the edge. I took my pleasure from him until we were both a sweaty, blood covered mess tangled on the bloodstained floor.

So quickly I couldn't register what was happening. He pinned me to the ground on my stomach, mounting me from behind. I don't know how he could keep going, but his cock sliding into my ass roughly had me seeing stars as I screamed out in a mix of pain and pleasure. He took from me without any remorse as he became a man unhinged.

I wasn't sure how long we stayed down here, but I was sure that after all the rounds we'd just gone and the multiple orgasms that a good deal of time had passed. We were a mass of tangled limbs, simply laying on this bloodstained floor, while we struggled to catch our breaths. My head lay on his chest, listening to his drumming heart rate slow as we came down from our high. His fingers lightly brushed through my hair. At this moment, I was content and completely satisfied.

Following what had happened in the basement, I'd needed a change of clothes before work. Damon really had become an animal because my clothes were completely ruined. The only thing that was saved from his wrath was my skirt. Sadly, there wasn't much to choose from as far as clothes here at the club. Damon had offered me an oversized shirt he had in his office and we had taken the time to clean up in a shower that he had downstairs. We made our way back up to open the club for the night once we were bathed of the blood and smell of sex. Nothing was said between us about what I had seen down in the basement or what had happened between us. It was probably best that we let it go.

The night was a slow one with just Zack and me working the bar with our couple of usual who just sort of hung around every night. It seemed like time was dragging on and I couldn't help when my eyes would roam to watch Damon if he was at the bar or on the floor mingling with the customers. My head really wasn't in the game today.

"So, what's the deal between you two?" Zack spoke right into my ear, causing me to jump.

"What the fuck Zack?" I squealed, backing away from him so that I could face him.

A wide smile spread across his face as he laughed at my expense and I smacked him across the back of the head lightly.

"Alright asshole, what do you want?" I said, rolling my eyes and going back to finishing the drink I was working on.

"What's going on between you and Damon, sweetness?" He said, leaning up against the bar while drying his hands with his rag.

I couldn't help it as I glanced back at Damon, who was up talking to the DJ. "Nothing is going on with us."

"I'm not so sure about that. You two haven't been able to keep your eyes off each other all night." He smiled, tossing his dirty rag at my face.

I caught it, tossing it to the counter beside me and didn't even bother to say anything back. If I was being honest, I wasn't even sure what was going on between us. There was definitely attraction, but was it possible it could be more than that? There was a pull between us I couldn't deny, but I refused to think it was anything more than physically. I had no intention of being one of those women that fell for a guy simply to end up disappointed in the end. I didn't see a happy ever after in my future. This world was far too cruel for that bullshit.

CHAPTER NINETEEN

Angel

Monday came and went with things slowly getting back to normal. Cherry had gone back to her place once Dimitri had gotten back from his trip and I took a much needed break from work. It was nice to have some time to myself after how crazy things had been. It felt like a lifetime had passed, when honestly, it had only been about two months since I started working at Hellfire.

I took my time off to just relax in my apartment watching crap TV and reading some books that I'd been meaning to get to. I couldn't even remember the last time I'd had a day where something wasn't going on. I hadn't realized how in need I was for a few days to myself. I ate crap food and did whatever I felt like doing. I didn't have anywhere to be or any need to do anything for someone else. It was nice to just be me. Even when I didn't really know who I was outside of the self-proclaimed mission I'd had for the past eight years. When this last job was done, I'd worry about all of that.

On Thursday morning, I awoke to a knock on my door. I was getting really sick of these weekly flower deliveries. I'd have to remember to tell Damon to stop with the flowers because it was interrupting my days to sleep in. Strolling to the door in nothing except my lacy panties and a fitted tank top, I slung the door open to come face to face with the man himself.

"I hope this isn't how you open the door for everyone, Angel." He said, trailing his eyes along every bit of exposed flesh.

I wasn't about to give him the satisfaction that he'd gotten to me by covering up, so I stood there bracing a hand on the door frame as I shamelessly eyed him as well. His hair was down in long, light brown waves today, a fitted white t-shirt that hugged his muscular chest and arms in all the right places, a pair of faded ripped jeans slung low on his hips, and black biker boots. Fuck, I could jump him right now.

"I have nothing to hide." I retorted, stepping back to allow him inside. The sooner he got in here, the sooner I could have those pants off him.

He walked inside and his enormous frame looked even larger in my small apartment. "I don't appreciate you showing off what belongs to me."

His eyes leveled me with a heated glare, but I didn't back down. "I don't fucking belong to you or anyone else."

He smiled as if he didn't believe me and started walking around my apartment as if interested in the few belongings that I had. I made a habit of not getting comfortable here because I knew it would all be temporary in the end. Once the last name was crossed off my list, I would disappear.

"You're going to need to pack up your things. You'll be living at the estate until further notice." He said in that deep voice that rumbled in his broad chest.

At his words, I clenched my fists at my sides. I knew by the hint of anger in his voice that he didn't like this either. He was simply the messenger. I knew who was trying to order me around, but it didn't lessen my anger.

Through gritted teeth, I said, "Fine."

"One other thing," He turned to look at me and strode up to me, slipping his hand into my hair pulling me flush against him, "what we've had has to end. My father is staking his claim. I don't want to see you hurt."

I had been wondering when Madax would want me all to himself, but I couldn't help the way my heart felt, like it was in a vice grip. "There wasn't ever anything between us, Damon."

He didn't waste a second as he pulled me into a searing kiss. This one was different from the rest. It was calmer and felt more intimate. I felt myself melting into him as I wrapped my arms around his neck, pulling him closer to me as we kissed. His tongue glided across my lips and I opened to let him in, moaning as he explored my mouth and our tongues fought for dominance. If this was going to be the last time, I wanted to make it memorable.

Pushing on his chest lightly, I backed him up until the back of his knees hit the bed, forcing him to topple onto the mattress as I climbed up to straddle him, never breaking the kiss. Our hands roamed each other as if we hadn't spent the last few months naked together. It was all so different compared to what we'd already shared. I didn't like this feeling. I didn't like that he was making me feel things at all.

Without warning, he flipped us, positioning himself between my legs as he kissed his way down my neck, to my collarbone, and to my breasts that were still confined in my shirt. His teeth bit at my already peaked nipple through the fabric, causing me to arch and moan out breathlessly. Taking his time before switching to give the other the same attention. He was worshiping my body in the best possible way and, for the first time; he was taking his time.

This was far from our usually fucking. We typically were frenzied and just simply at that point where things were primal. This was different. If I wasn't in complete denial about it, I would call this *making love*. That thought alone made a surge of panic wash over me. I don't know if I said something out loud or if he just knew my body that well, but he changed his pace at the same time that panic gripped me.

He removed my panties in a single, fluid motion and settled himself between my legs. He kissed up from my knee to inner thigh, to the D he'd cut into my skin. It was nothing more than a branded scar at this point. His tongue darted out to run along the jagged lines of the mark and I moaned softly at the feeling. I had never been owned before, but there was no denying in these stolen moments, I was his. I'd never admit that to anyone else, especially not to him.

My thoughts shattered as he ran that devilish tongue up my slit until he reached my clit, working that bundle of nerves until I was gripping his hair tightly in my hands and grinding against his sinful mouth. Fuck, he knew exactly what he was doing.

He was still taking his time, savoring every curse and moan to escape my lips, until I screamed as a fast wave of ecstasy overtook me. I tightened my thighs around his head and rode his face as the waves of pleasure took over until I was panting and sated. He wasn't done with me yet though, and I was completely at his mercy.

CHAPTER TWENTY

Damon

Never in my life had I made love to a woman, but here I was with Angel's sweet release on my tongue as she came down from her high. I knew this wouldn't be my last time with her. She was mine, but it felt right. It felt needed as she completely submitted to me in these moments.

I ran my tongue up her glistening cunt once more before standing to remove my clothes. She was the most beautiful thing I'd ever seen as she laid there watching me with hooded eyes. Her cold eyes were the brightest blue I'd ever seen as I watched her eyes trail down to my cock. I towered over her small frame. She was so small in comparison and it had a fucking twisted way of making me want to protect her. Without a second thought, I crawled back onto the bed and fitted myself between her luscious thighs. I kissed her deeply as I slipped my cock into her tight pussy and groaned at the feeling of her wrapped around me. So wet and so warm. She was mine.

I pumped my hips in a slow, leisurely pace as I made love to this beautiful woman. There was nothing rough or primal about this as I pushed her knees to her chest, forcing myself deeper and giving her the friction she'd need to come, even at my slow pace. I wanted her to feel all of me and know who it was she belonged to. She needed to know that she was cared for, even while locked in that house with a veritable monster.

Angel had insisted that I allow her to drive her car back to the estate. I was hesitant since my father had made it clear she couldn't simply come and go as she pleased. I'd explained that little fact to her and yet she still insisted. It was hard to argue with her with that look of determination on her face.

With her bags packed, we both headed back to the estate and got her settled into the same room as before. She went about setting her things where she wanted, putting her clothes away in the closet and dresser. I sat on the bed in silence as I watched her make herself at home. The last thing she did was pull out a knife and a roll of duct tape from her bag and headed over to the headboard. I didn't ask questions as she taped the knife to the back of the headboard to her liking, where it was hidden. I was intrigued to know why she'd done it, but I knew better than to question her. Once she was done, she sat down on the bed next to me and began absentmindedly picking at the threads of the white duvet.

"Does everything have to be fucking white?" She asked without glancing up at me.

A quiet, gruff laugh left my chest at her comment as I stood up to leave. Before I could take a step away, she grabbed onto my hand and I looked down at her in surprise. I tightened my hand around hers and simply said, "Angel, you could burn this world down to ash without the help of anyone else and I'd simply watch in awe."

Kissing the knuckles of her hand lightly. "I won't be around much anymore. I'll be staying away at my penthouse near the bar, but if you need anything, you have my number."

Walking out of that room and leaving her felt like the weight of the world rested on my shoulders. All I wanted to do was stay by her side and keep her from having to deal with my fucked up father. I knew she could handle herself, but that didn't mean I didn't want to be there within reach if she ever needed me. With my stomach in knots, I hopped in my car and drove off, leaving my Angel at the hands of the devil himself.

CHAPTER TWENTY-ONE

Angel

It was so weird being in this house all alone. Madax wasn't here due to work, so it left me on my own as I searched the house and learned all the exits should I ever need them. I hadn't expected Damon to not be here, and I hated the empty feeling in my gut from his absence. Why the fuck did I feel like I needed him around? I'd been on my own for the past eight years, so I knew I didn't need Damon or anyone else.

This had all been part of the plan. To get Madax alone and earn his trust. What better way to get my revenge than to be in the same house where he slept? This would make it so much easier to kill him when it was convenient for me. I'd just need to make sure no one of importance knew I'd been staying here with him. On my walk around the house, I had hidden plenty of weapons. I hid knives and guns where only I would know their locations. Now I was just counting down the clock to when I could take Madax out for good.

As night fell, I went to the kitchen to prepare a meal for myself and made extra in case Madax came home early. I sat my phone on the counter to listen to music while I worked on the dinner. I helped myself to a bottle of red wine, drinking it as I cooked. The heat from the alcohol in my system had me relaxing in this uncomfortable space.

"I didn't expect to come home to this, but I can't say I'm not intrigued." A gruff voice said from the entry to the kitchen.

I jumped, spinning around to see Madax standing there, slinging his suit jacket onto the back of one of the bar stools. "Shit, you scared me."

He smiled as he took a seat at the kitchen island and poured himself a glass of wine. "Sorry about that, darling. What are you making?"

"I thought you might be hungry after work, so I'm making spaghetti," I said, taking another sip of my wine as he eyed me like prey, "I'm not the best cook, but it's one of the few things I know how to make."

"I love spaghetti." He said simply, his eyes staying far too long on my cleavage available to him with my low cut t-shirt.

I turned around and went about finishing up the dinner, putting it on plates, and served him his first. I topped off his wine, then took a seat next to him. We ate in silence, other than him complimenting me on the spaghetti. Once we finished our meals, I cleaned up the plates and glasses, rinsed them in the sink, and placed them in the dishwasher, along with everything else I'd used to make dinner.

When I finished cleaning up the kitchen, he took my hand, and I followed him into the sitting room. There was a large TV that filled up one wall and a bar on the opposite end of the room. A set up of matching white chairs and couches lined the room in between them. I assumed he wanted to watch TV, since this was the room he brought me to. He sat me down and handed me the remote, telling me to pick whatever I wanted to watch, while he went over to the bar to get himself a glass of scotch. He sat down next to me on the couch, pulling me closer so that he could wrap his arms around me. We got comfortable, or as comfortable as I could be, in his arms, as we sat down and I turned on a slasher flick. Slasher and horror movies were some of my favorites. Even I could admit that Ghost-face in the original Scream was pretty hot. That scene where he licked the "blood" from his fingers just did something for me. I was a sick fuck for finding murder hot.

"I'm glad you came to stay with me, darling. I didn't expect you to be so *domesticated* though," Madax whispered in his deep tenor, trailing his fingers lightly down my arm.

I tilted my head back on his shoulder to smile at him sweetly. What I really wanted to do was make him scream out in pain, but I didn't say that or let it show on my face as we settled back down to finish the movie. His hands slipped down my body, finding their way under my shirt and into my panties from time to time. Despite him being so touchy he didn't force himself on me, which I was grateful for.

CHAPTER TWENTY-TWO

Angel

My gratitude from the night before was short-lived. I'd made my way downstairs the next morning setting out to make myself a light breakfast of eggs and avocado on toast, Letting the coffee brew while I worked at the stove to cook the eggs. I didn't turn to look as Madax made his way inside the kitchen. I'd already placed his newspaper that had been delivered on the counter where he took a seat and began reading while I finished plating the breakfast and making us both cups of coffee.

We sat in silence enjoying our breakfast, but my body remained stiff being so close to him. My skin crawled and all I wanted to do was reach over to grab one of the kitchen knives. To feel it sink into his eye socket, for his blood to coat my hands. Instead I finished off my breakfast and took out empty dishes over to the sink to rinse. All while daydreaming about all the ways I could kill Madax. How I'd relish holding his life in my hands while he bleed out before me.

I was so deep in my head that I didn't notice when said man came up behind me, wrapping his arms around me to turn the water off.

"I had hoped you would come to me last night." Disappointment leaked from his words as his hand skated down my stomach and into the waistband of my leggings. His fingers found my clit and worked me in a slow rhythm.

I tensed in his hold as he ground his hard dick into me from behind. No noises of pleasure left me as I breathed through my nose, nearly choking on the smell of his cologne. A growl left his lips. Someone wasn't a fan that he couldn't make me scream or beg. With a strength I wasn't expecting he bent me over the sink, his hand fisting in my hand while his other pushed my pants down enough to leave me exposed. I deftly heard the sound of his zipper before he plunged into me. Fucking me in a way that wasn't meant for my pleasure. He took and my nails dug into the edges of the sink. The knives were too far out of reach. My eyes trailed to the plates and mugs? Could I break one fast enough and bury the shard of china into his jugular? No, that wasn't an option. Dimitri already warned me that he was working on something behind the scenes of all this. I couldn't kill him yet. Fuck!

All I could do was take it while he rutted into me like a senseless beast. His hand tightening in my hair as he grunted out his release. I hoped he would leave me to go wash myself, but he held me in place. His hand moved from my hair to trail down my arm while he placed gentle kisses on my shoulder and neck.

"I'll be busy this week, darling. I hope you'll have breakfast with me every morning." He ground against me as he spoke. His come leaking down my thighs in a sticky mess.

I couldn't speak. My tone would give me away, so I simply nodded. With one final kiss to my shoulder he pulled away from me, fastened his pants, and left me alone to clean up his mess.

First things first, a long hot shower.

Things continued fairly smoothly over the next couple of weeks. I worked nights at the club and found Madax already in bed when I got back to the estate from my shifts. To be completely honest, I didn't really see him that often, and I was perfectly fine with that. He made time for just the two of us to have breakfast. His favorite part of breakfast was bending more over the kitchen counter to fuck me until he was coming in me. He didn't fuck me for my pleasure, that was certain. Overall, the experience of living with the man I was going to kill wasn't all that complicated.

Damon had been avoiding me even at work, and I wasn't sure how I felt about that. He would only speak to me if completely necessary, but I had caught him staring at me throughout the evenings I worked. A part of me couldn't stand the distance that was between us, even though I knew this was all temporary. He'd wormed his way under my skin and I hated him for it.

Madax had mentioned wanting to take me out on a "proper date" this weekend, and I felt it would be the perfect time to go through with ending all of this. I'd need to run it by Damon to make sure I was off Saturday night and that we were on the same page. Things had to be done right. I wasn't going down over something stupid. Orange just wasn't my color. I knew Dimitri had meant it when he said he'd throw me to the wolves if need be. It was time to end this.

CHAPTER TWENTY-THREE

Damon

I was sitting at my desk at the end of the night talking to Dimitri, when in walked my favorite little play thing. She'd worn a fitted black dress tonight that left little to the imagination and all I could think about was bending her over my desk to slide my dick into her welcoming little cunt.

She hadn't even bothered to knock as she walked into my office and plopped her fine ass down in the chair next to Dimitri. "Hi boys, just wanted to let you know I plan on finishing this shit tomorrow night. Damon, I need tomorrow off, but leave me on the schedule as an alibi."

Dimitri blinked at her in surprise, while I just smiled at her. She had held out longer than I thought possible since I dropped her off. I had honestly expected to find out my father was dead within the first week, but my Angel was smart and liked to fuck with her prey, apparently. I could respect that.

"What's the plan, baby girl?" I said, leaning back in my chair.

She just smiled before telling us her plan. I had to admit it was well planned out and it would be quick. The only thing she needed from us was a quick cleanup and an alibi. I'd simply say she had been at work for the entire night and we'd spent the night working at the club as usual. With the help of Jensen, I'd be able to cover us with video footage showing her in the club. The plan was set and by tomorrow night, we'd have the keys to the kingdom.

Once we were done talking over the details of her plan, Angel excused herself and headed home for the night. Dimitri sat silently throughout the entire conversation, and I was interested in hearing his thoughts.

"It's a good plan, but I still don't trust her." He said, pulling a cigarette from his pocket and lighting it.

"She saved your girl's ass. The least we can do is back her up a bit. I know you don't get your hands dirty.

So, let her handle the messy business and we will take care of cleaning up together." I said, lighting a smoke.

Things could go south fast, but I was confident about Angel and her plan.

CHAPTER TWENTY-FOUR

Angel

I awoke this morning feeling refreshed and completely energized. Today was the day everything I'd been working for over the past eight years would end. I'd finally get revenge for Jessica and I'd be able to move on with my life. I wouldn't be stuck in this hellhole of a city that brought so much pain to my life.

Climbing out of bed, I made my way into the bathroom to get myself showered and ready for the day. I took extra time to shave and exfoliate in the shower, to moisturize so my skin was soft and glowy, curled my long, black hair into waves that perfectly framed my face, and applied a light makeup look with my favorite red lipstick.

Today was already starting out to be a good day. I walked out of the bathroom in my black silk robe to find an arrangement of gifts laid out on my bed. It included a white body-con dress that would fall to just above my knees, a pair of silver, red bottom heels, a single red rose, and a note from Madax.

I didn't want to interrupt your shower this morning, so I'm just leaving these here for you. There are a lot of things I would love to do with you. I'll see you soon. ~ Madax

Rolling my eyes at the note, I quickly dressed in what he had laid out for me. I took it upon myself to pair it with a red lacy thong. I knew exactly how tonight would end, and I needed the old fuck salivating for me before it was over.

The day had started out fairly well. Madax took me to a nice breakfast, where they served a large spread of food along with bottomless mimosas. To say I was tipsy afterward was an understatement, but Madax was a perfect gentleman as we made our way to the next thing he had planned. We walked around an art gallery where he explained how he knew the artist who created most of the works, to the mall for some shopping, a light lunch on the pier where the restaurant, which was suspended over the rolling waves, and we ended the night at a five-star restaurant where they served an 8 course meal.

Madax had spoiled me today and shown off the type of lifestyle he could provide for me. I was certain he wanted to move things along far more quickly than I was ready for with anyone. I played along, swooning over everything he did and said. By the end of the night, we had made it back to the estate after a fairly nice day together. I'd worked my charms to get him as flustered as I could throughout the day, and caused him to tent his slacks at the most awkward moments. My plan to seduce him tonight was working out perfectly.

He took the time to escort me to my room, and I took the chance to push things in the direction I'd wanted. This was my chance, and I wouldn't waste another moment stuck in this house with this rotten man. I opened the door to my room and turned to face him.

"Care to spend the evening with me?" I asked suggestively, dragging my nails slightly down his chest. I could feel his lean muscles rippling underneath his dress shirt and jacket.

"I've wanted to feel your pretty cunt wrapped around me all day, darling." He said, peppering kisses along my neck.

"Then take me to bed, Madax." I forced myself to sound husky.

He was acting like a starved man and I could tell his hunger only grew at my words when he looked at me. His eyes were nearly black with his need. All I hungered for was his death.

He picked me up, and I wrapped my legs around his waist. He was already hard and I could feel the length fitted against my core. I kissed him to force back the gag I desperately wanted to let slip. This man was disgusting in every sense of the word. The world would be a much better place without him and his influence on it.

He carried me a short distance to the bed, tossing me onto the plush duvet. These white linens would look so much better covered in red. I didn't understand why he adored the color so much, much like this ugly dress he had me in.

I watched as he unbuckled his gray slacks and freed his cock. I couldn't help thinking how much bigger his son was. That must have been why he fought so hard to "steal" me away from Damon. The prick had an ego and while he had allowed me my fun with Damon, it had obviously pissed him off. I sat up on the bed, sliding my red lacy thong off in one fluid motion.

He stood proud and naked before me, before pushing me back onto the bed, fitting himself between my legs. He kissed me savagely as he positioned himself at my entrance. I spread my legs farther, wrapping them around his waist as he plunged into me. He obviously couldn't tell how much I loathed his touch. He didn't make me wet in the slightest. Then again, he probably couldn't tell the difference with how many girls he'd forced himself inside.

I simply went through the motions of moaning and thrusting my hips to match his pace. I could feel his breath on my neck as he trailed kisses towards my breasts. His hand moved between us to stroke my clit while he thrust his dick deep inside me. I couldn't stop the real moan from leaving my lips as my pussy clenched around him. I hated that my body couldn't get the message. That it had the audacity to like what he did to it. I only loathed him more for that fact. Every nerve in my body was wound tight as I came on his cock. My back arching from the sheer force as Madax continued to fuck me through my orgasm. I felt dirty and couldn't stand the feeling of him inside of me, making my body answer to him, and I wanted it all to end. I couldn't take this much longer. As quickly as I could, I flipped us, positioning myself to ride him.

He simply smirked up at me, "So impatient."

I smiled down at him, riding him faster. He groaned out in pleasure, throwing his head back and closed his eyes.

"Just like that, baby. Make Daddy come in your pretty little cunt."

It would be the last orgasm he ever had. I lifted myself, forcing him into me repeatedly as he bucked his hips up to meet my thrusts. He was so close, so I rolled my hips, giving him a bit more friction until he came, groaning out his release as he filled me.

At my chance, I slipped my hand over the edge of the headboard, wrapping my hand around the hilt of my knife. As quickly as I could, I released it from its holster and slashed it across his throat. His eyes flew open and bulged wide as he reached for his throat. Gurgling as he choked on his own blood. I climbed off of him while he fought for his final breaths. Taking a moment, I readjusted my white, now splattered red dress. I could feel our combined release dripping down my thighs. I really needed a fucking shower.

"That's for Jessica." I whispered, making my way out of the room. Never taking a second longer to look back as Madax gasped for the last time. Death had finally come for the last name on my list. It was fucking over.

CHAPTER TWENTY-FIVE

Damon

I stood leaning against the wall, smoking my fifth cigarette within the past hour. I'd spent the night with my bike parked just in view of the house so that I'd know when it was done. Once they'd entered the house, I'd slipped inside and waited here outside Angel's bedroom door. The noises they were making were enough to piss me off, even though I knew it was all fake on Angel's part. The door opened and god, Angel was a sight. Seeing her exit that room in her white, fitted dress covered in blood was probably the hottest thing I'd ever laid eyes on. She held her knife in one hand and a lace thong dangled from the fingertips of her other. She looked like a bloody angel of death and my dick strained against my zipper.

She smiled upon seeing me standing there and extended the panties towards me. "I believe these belong to you."

I smirked around my cigarette, grabbed her around the waist, pulling her against me. "I think I already have what belongs to me right here."

I plucked the panties from her hand, stuffing them in my back pocket.

She glared up at me and placed her knife against my throat. "I belong to no man."

If looks could kill, I'd be a rotting corpse. Instead, all I wanted to do was fuck her here in this hall. Just the thought had me growing painfully hard. I slipped my hand into her dark, midnight hair, forcing her face closer to mine. I discarded my cigarette and smiled down at her beautiful face.

"Keep telling yourself that, baby girl."

I quickly picked her up with one arm and twisted us, forcing her back against the wall. In the rush, she dropped her knife, and I took the chance to kiss her shamelessly. She wrapped her legs around me and ground against my cock. Fuck, she was already soaking and I could feel the heat seeping into my jeans. My Angel was always ready for me. Reaching between us, she made quick work of freeing my cock and positioned it at the entrance of her dripping wet pussy. I needed no other invitation and thrust into her, hard. She moaned loudly against my lips and rocked her hips to match my pounding thrusts. I could die a happy man with her cunt strangling my cock.

I increased my pace, fucking her ruthlessly. She threw her head back against the wall, moaning my name towards the ceiling. She was already so close for me. Moving one hand from around her thigh, I lightly wrapped it around her slender throat, increasing the pressure slightly. I could already feel her pussy tightening around my cock. I slowed my pace just enough to keep her on the edge.

"Who do you belong to, Angel?" I growled in her ear.

I could feel her take a shallow breath. Almost like she was fighting with herself, which I'm sure she was. I slowed my pace farther and what could only be considered a growl formed in her throat. It only made my grin widen, and I bit into the tender flesh below her ear. She thread her fingers into my hair, pulling hard enough to force me from her neck. Fuck, my angel was so hot when she was pissed. I slammed my cock deeper into her welcoming cunt and a loud, pleasured moan escaped her lips, forcing her eyes to roll. I simply smirked at her and repeated the question.

"Who do you belong to?" I emphasized each word with a hard thrust of my hips. I knew I sounded demanding, but I needed to hear her say the words.

"You!" she screamed at me, digging her nails deeper into my skin. "Now let me come, asshole."

She didn't have to tell me twice. I'd gotten what I wanted. I jack hammered into her tight pussy, fucking her hard and fast. Oh, so quickly she came undone in my arms. Screaming my name as her cunt gushed around me. Angel dug her nails into my scalp as wave after wave of pleasure assaulted her, but she would find no mercy from me. I continued my hard thrusts and slipped my hand between us, massaging her clit just the way she liked it. She came again in an instant. I loved how responsive her body was to my ministrations and I planned to use her up for the rest of the night.

When I was done with Angel for the time being, I dropped her off at her apartment and headed back to the estate. Dimitri was already there leaning against the hood of his car with a ring of smoke circling his head from his half finishing cigarette. I parked my bike right next to him, cutting the engine and tossing my helmet on the handle.

"You're late." He said, cutting his eyes at me, which only made me smile.

"I had to make sure my girl was tucked in. She's had a busy day." I grinned, kicking the stand down before throwing my leg over the side of the bike to stand in front of him.

He rolled his eyes and walked towards the front door. "Grab those cans out of the trunk and let's get this over with."

I did as he said and hauled the cans of gas inside. We took our time covering each floor and the body in gasoline before making our way back out the front door. He didn't look back or say a word as he got back into his car and drove off. I didn't understand what was up his ass tonight. We'd gotten what we wanted, and he'd soon be the big man on top.

I pulled out a cigarette and match, striking it on the side of the door frame. Once I lit my smoke, I tossed the match into the foyer and the white rugs erupted into flames. I made my way back to my bike and drove a little way from the estate. Far enough that I wouldn't be noticed when the authorities showed up, yet still close enough to watch the action.

The place was engulfed in flames by the time anyone showed up. There was little else other than the foundation left once they put the fires out. I wish that Angel could have been here to see the masterpiece, but she had insisted that I drop her off at her place. I only stayed until people were sent out to see what was left. They wouldn't find any traces of my father, so there was nothing else to look forward to watching. I mounted my bike and headed back to Angel's place, as the sun was just beginning to rise in the distance.

CHAPTER TWENTY-SIX

Angel

Damon had been gone most of the night, which gave me just enough time to pack up the few bags I could fit on my bike. I was hoping to be gone before he had gotten back, but I heard the door click open as I was throwing the last bag over my shoulder.

"Well, this wasn't what I'd been expecting from you, Angel." He said as his boots pounded the tile floor on his way over to me.

I couldn't outrun him, so I turned to face him head on. "The keys to the car and apartment are on the counter. It's yours. I won't be needing it."

His usual smug look wasn't on his face as he reached up to push a strand of hair behind my ear. "Angel, no matter how far you try to run, you'll always come back to me. You're mine."

I didn't have the heart to lie and tell him he was wrong. I admitted as much last night. That didn't mean I had to stay. I wasn't interested in a happily ever after sort of life. I had spent so many years getting revenge on the men who had hurt Jessica and now I felt hollow. I needed to figure out what my life could be now that it was mine.

Damon didn't need to know any of that, so I simply grabbed the collar of his shirt, pulling him down to me for one last kiss. We poured everything into that last kiss as his arms engulfed me, pulling me so close I felt as if he was trying to mold us into one being. The kiss was desperate and savage.

I couldn't tell him goodbye. I didn't have it in me. So I pulled away, leaving just a hand on his chest, and looked him in the eye. I hoped everything I couldn't say he knew from looking at me. With a final pat to his chest, I walked around him and out of my former apartment building. I didn't look back as I strapped my bags to my bike before straddling the beautiful machine and throwing my helmet on. I knew he was standing there watching me.

So I waved my hand slightly in the air before driving off
into the unknown.

CHAPTER TWENTY-SEVEN

Damon

It had been about three months since everything had gone down and I'd watched Angel drive off. Dimitri had taken over the business and had the fire brushed off as something ridiculous, like a gas leak. Our father had been inside sleeping when the fire engulfed the house, leaving his death ruled an accident.

Angel had been completely M.I.A., at least to me. She'd only spoken to Cherry since leaving. The last Cherry had heard from her was a month ago. She was somewhere on the East coast and she was happy. She could live her fantasy for a little while longer. I had people looking into her whereabouts. I was going to bring her back home, even if I had to drag her back kicking and screaming myself.

"You know they are going to retaliate, eventually. Our father was their biggest supporter, and you cut them off a month ago." I said, taking a sip of my scotch.

Dimitri threw a glare my way before resuming his typing on his computer. He'd been doing amazing with the business since taking over and I had to admit it seemed right that he was now sitting at the boss's desk.

"It has been a month. I don't know what they are planning, but I know it's coming. Everyone is on alert and we will deal with it when it happens."

I scoffed, sitting my tumbler on the desk. "You say that now."

Before he could say anything else, Zack came bursting through the doors. He was panting, and he seemed oddly pale considering his usual tan.

"They took her." He gasped out in a panic.

Dimitri's fingers paused over the keys as he looked at Zack with horror etched on his face. Zack had sunk to the floor just inside the door, and I knew what I needed to do.

Without saying a word to either of them, I pulled out my phone and dialed the number of the one person I knew would know exactly what to do. She answered after only one ring.

"They took Cherry."

CHAPTER TWENTY-EIGHT

Angel

Blood pounded in my ears as I stood there on the balcony of my apartment. The ocean waves and songs of seabirds filled the silence as I processed what Damon had just said.

They took Cherry. They as in the fuckers who'd been stealing girls in my old city. The same people Madax had been working with and who Dimitri ended deals with as soon as he took over. I wanted to punch the damn wall as anger flooded my system.

I should have known better. Should have known that I couldn't run from my old life forever. I'd just spoken with Cherry yesterday and I thought everything was fine.

Cherry had reassured me that things had been quiet. That I didn't have anything to worry about.

Now I was getting a call from the last person I wanted to talk to. I hadn't spoken to Damon since that last day with him three months ago. I hadn't looked back. I'd driven off into the rising sun and pretended like that part of my life never happened. I'd finally settled down on the banks of North Carolina. Found myself working odd jobs while I focused on trying to figure out what I wanted my life to look like. Go figure something would happen to drag me back to that place.

"I'll be there soon."

I didn't wait for a response. Hanging up the phone and stalking into my apartment. I'd need to pack a bag and head out as soon as possible. The longer it took me to get there the harder it would be to track down where those fuckers took Cherry.

CHAPTER TWENTY-NINE

Angel

"It's a good plan and I don't need your fucking permission."

Damon stood in front of me, bitching about my plan to get Cherry back. Dimitri was no fucking help, that was for sure. He sat there on the plush couch, looking completely broken. He nursed a tumbler filled with whatever he could get his hands on and there was a good amount of stubble on his usually clean-shaven face. I didn't think he'd ever let himself go like this, but I also couldn't blame him, given the situation.

"It's a shit plan. You'll be on your own." Damon growled, towering over me.

His sweet mahogany scent wrapped around me, making me feel needy and suffocated at the same time. It had been far too long since I'd been laid and tensions were high at the moment. I wasn't an idiot and wouldn't let myself fall back into bed with the asshole this time around. I barely got out last time and I was positive I couldn't do it again.

"It's a good plan, Damon. She could get in easily and make sure Cherry was safe. If we can track her, we will know exactly where she is and we can make a plan to get them both out." Zack said.

Damon just growled, shooting a glare at his friend. He was really going to get on my fucking nerves. I'd been gone for months and now he wanted to be this overprotective asshole when we had other things to worry about. We needed Dimitri to snap the fuck out of it, and we needed to get everything prepared so that we could get Cherry back.

Walking over to Dimitri, I snatched the drink from his hands and downed what was left in the glass. He glared up at me from his seat and I got directly into his face. "I get it. This is a shit situation, but pouting like a fucking child isn't helping her. Man, the fuck up."

His bloodshot eyes continued to glare at me. "Do whatever you have to do to get her back. You'll have access to all our money and resources."

His words were slurred as he got up from the couch and stumbled out of the room. With one last glare at me, Damon walked out after his brother. Leaving just Zack and me in the lounge. Zack was the only one who was keeping a level head, mostly. I knew he was falling apart, but he was focused on us getting his sister back. His focus would come in handy for getting things prepared. We couldn't afford for everyone to lose their shit.

"I'm going to need the contacts of the people who can help us," I said, collapsing on the couch next to him.

"I'll get them for you, sweetness." He said without looking at me.

I placed my hand on his knee, giving him a comforting pat. "I'm going to get her back, Zack. They fucked with the wrong people."

We spent the rest of the night going over everything that needed to be done, Damon only returning as we finished up for the night. He gave Zack a pat on the back as he walked past, shutting the door behind him. I did my best not to look at the man who'd been the star of my best dreams these past months, as he moved further into the room. Nursing my tumbler as I watched the people down below on the floor of Hellfire. It had been so long since I'd worked those very floors. Almost a lifetime ago. I'd run off as soon as Madax was dealt with and I'd had no intention of ever coming back to this life. There were too many skeletons in the closet. Too much bad blood to build a decent life here. I had needed to find my own place in the world, no matter what I was leaving behind to deal with in the aftermath.

Damon sighed as he took a seat next to me on the sofa, taking the tumbler from my hand to place on the coffee table. "I was still drinking that."

"We need to talk." Damon's gruff voice sounded exhausted before his hand found its way around my throat, forcing me to look at him directly.

A part of me wanted to slit his throat, and yet another wanted him to take me right here. "Get the fuck off me."

My voice dripped with venom and heat as I glared up into his blue eyes, letting my eyes trail down the length of his face. He'd trimmed his beard since I'd seen him last, but it was still long, surrounding his full lips that I knew could bring me immense pleasure. Yeah, it had definitely been too long since I'd been fucked. Now that I think about it, Damon was the last time.

A wicked smirk lit up Damon's face as his hand tightened around my throat. "Play nice, Angel, and I'll let you come."

My heart raced in my chest as I pulled the knife from my boot, holding it to his throat. The feeling of déjà vu washed over me. He always liked to play these sorts of games. Damon's other hand wrapped around my wrist until I was forced to drop my blade. He pushed me by my throat, forcing me onto my back where he hovered over me and I wasn't able to reach him or my weapon.

"That's not nice, Angel." His voice morphed into a deep growl in his chest, and heat pulled at my core from the sound alone.

I moved to scratch my nails down the forearm, keeping me pinned until something cold brushed up my inner thigh, right next to the crudely carved D. This man had branded me the last time I'd been in a similar situation like this. Looking down, my blade was held in his large hand, blood already dripping from his palm as he trailed the hilt under the hem of my skirt.

"What the fuck do you think you're doing?" I forced every ounce of hate I possessed into my voice, bucking and clawing to free myself. Nothing made him budge as the hilt found my entrance. Why had I not worn anything underneath this skirt tonight? The cold metal moved up at an agonizing pace to the bundle of nerves at the apex of my thighs, stimulating until I was panting and my fight dissolved. It was so hard to fight Damon when I was trying not to show him the effect he had on me.

CHAPTER THIRTY

Damon

It had been too long. Regardless of what we were facing, I needed to bury myself in her cunt. Angel had always had a way of getting under my skin. Every part of me wanted to feel her underneath me. For her scent to surround me as I brought us both to release. She'd pissed me off earlier, and I wanted to take that anger out on her like my own personal toy.

Now that she was beneath me, panting, her thighs spread while I worked her clit with the cold metal of her knife. My hand flared in pain where I gripped the blade, but it only fueled my need to fill her. So much hatred shone in her cold, blue eyes and I took my time to play with her, to admire my little Angel. More tattoos decorated her skin since I'd last seen her. A piece peeking out from between her breast that I wanted to see the extent of what covered her below her sweater. A rose peaked out of the collar, taking up the entire right side of her slender neck. My cock ached, pushing against my zipper as I took her in.

Without warning, I slammed the hilt of the knife into her dripping wet cunt, tearing a moan from her ruby-red lips. Her head tossed back onto the couch as I fucked her with her own knife. I smiled to myself as she came around the knife; her release mixing with my blood that now covered her thighs. Pulling the knife free, I finally tossed it onto the coffee table and let go of her throat. Watching her chest rise and fall as she tried to catch her breath.

I didn't expect my Angel to want me. Not after she'd run off the last time, avenging her dead sister. I was pleasantly surprised when she lashed out, gripping me by my jacket to pull me into a heated kiss. There was never anything soft about this woman. She took what she wanted and had no intention of caring about anyone else. My hands tangled in her long black hair as she straddled me, her skirt bunched around her hips as she ground against my length, soaking my jeans in the process.

Angel reached between our bodies, working quickly to free my cock, her hands working the length as she positioned herself above me. Our mouths and tongues fought for dominance while she slid down my cock, her warm cunt strangling me as she slid down to the base, forcing me as deep as possible into her heat.

I groaned against her lips, my hands finding her hips as she began to ride me. "That's a good girl. Let that perfect cunt strangle my cock."

She bit at my lip, thrusting her hips faster and I fucked up into her core. Using my hands to slam her down on my cock until I could feel my balls tightening. At this rate, I wasn't going to last long for my little Angel. That wouldn't do. Without missing a beat, I pushed her back onto the floor, thrusting my cock back into her at a punishing speed. Her body arched into mine as her legs wrapped around my waist and she met my thrusts with her own.

Wrapping a hand around her throat, forcing her to look at me and cutting off her air supply, "Come for me, Angel."

At my command, I felt her cunt tighten around me and a flood of heat coat my thighs. I loved how responsive she was to me. Spurring my hips faster until I was coming deep inside her. Holding her there, wishing my hands were enough to keep her here with me this time. I tried not to think of that as I pulled myself from her, flipping her over onto her hands and knees with her beautiful ass up in the air. From this angle I could see the D I'd carved into her creamy thigh, letting my finger lazily trace the crude scar. I wasn't going to let her get away this time, and I was far from done with her.

A rumbling growl left my lips as I sank into her again. "Mine."

CHAPTER THIRTY-ONE

Angel

I was sitting in a makeshift doctor's office in some warehouse off the docks. Of course, the Ashfords had their own personal doctor along with a long list of contacts who could help me get what I needed.

Zack had reached out to their tech guy, Jensen, who created a tracker, and *The Doctor* was going to implant it so that the boys could track me when I went into the lion's den, so to speak. Doc was an older gentleman who appeared to be in his early seventies as he prepped my neck for the implant. I'd made sure it would go on my left side. I didn't need a big ass scar on my new ink.

Wrinkles decorated his face, framing his chocolate brown eyes, and he had very little grey hair at this point. I watched as he meticulously got the needle contraption set up for the implant. It reminded me of those things they used to microchip dogs, but I guess that could be exactly what it was. I'm sure this guy wasn't an actual doctor, considering we were in a warehouse.

"This is going to sting a bit," He said in his aged, wispy voice as he pinched the skin on my neck.

"I'm not scared of a bit of pain, Doc." He hadn't offered me his name when I'd arrived and I wasn't in the mood to ask.

He plunged the oversized needle into my neck, causing me to flinch before he pulled the trigger. Nothing else was said as he slapped a bandage over the wound and sent me on my way. I hope he was good at what he did because he had shit bedside manner.

I made my way out of the warehouse into the salty air. I missed the smell of the water here. This place had been home before everything went to shit. If I closed my eyes for a second, I could pretend that all the awful shit hadn't happened. I'd had no intention of ever coming back to this shit hole, but I had to admit a part of me belonged here.

A horn honked in the distance, drawing my attention to my old Impala. It looked as if she'd been done up since the last time I'd seen her. I knew leaving the beautiful machine with Damon had been the right thing to do. He'd cleaned up my old car and had her fully restored. The black paint was shiny, and the only thing that gave away the fact that it had been mine at all was the chrome snake mascot on the front hood.

I walked over, running my hand along the hood as I passed, before slipping into the car and sinking into the worn leather seats. I closed my eyes and leaned my head back on the seat as Damon drove off.

"I couldn't bring myself to change your car," Damon said in that deep voice I'd dreamed so many months about. It was rough and sent shivers over my skin in the most delectable way.

"It's not mine anymore." I simply wasn't in the mood to argue, and the rest of the drive was silent.

He said he'd made arrangements for my stay while I was here. I didn't plan on staying once we got Cherry back and we could settle this crap with Madax's old partners, but I felt responsible in a way because I just took him out and ran away. I didn't stick around to see what the aftermath would be or and now my friend had been taken. That twisted my gut. She was a sweet girl who didn't deserve what had happened, and I felt responsible. Just one more person I cared about that I'd failed to protect. I'd do whatever it took to get her back.

We pulled up to my old apartment building, and I glanced over as Damon cut the engine and got out. Why would he bring me here? I was positive he would have sold off my old place.

He didn't even look back to make sure I was following him as he entered the building. I got out of the car and followed him inside as he was making his way up the stairwell. Sure enough, he was opening the door to my old apartment when I made it to the top of the stairs. He left the door open and leaned against the doorframe as I made my way over to him. Stepping inside, I felt a rush of déjà vu. That feeling seemed to be a constant since coming back to my old life here. Nothing had been moved. It was exactly as I'd left it when I wanted out months ago. It had obviously been cleaned, but nothing was out of place. I walked over to my nightstand and found the book I'd started still laying face down to save the page I'd been on.

I heard the booted footsteps and the door shutting as Damon made his way inside while I was looking over everything. I made my way into the small kitchen area and opened the fridge to see that it had been freshly stocked. Including a selection of my favorite drinks. I pulled out two beers and popped the tops off on the counter as I walked over to Damon, offering him a drink. He took it without saying a word, lifting the bottle to his lips. Watching his arms flex and the way his throat bobbed as he took a swig shouldn't have been as sexy as it was. Standing this close to him, all I could smell was his manly scent, and I felt the need to clench my thighs together.

To distract myself, I turned to look around the small space once more while taking a swig of my beer. "You didn't change anything."

"I knew you'd come back eventually," was all he said as he made his way over to my small couch, where he took a seat and propped his booted heels on the scuffed-up coffee table.

I rolled my eyes before taking a seat next to him, leaving a bit of space between us. Things had been so awkward with us since I'd gotten back. The heat was still there, but it was as if something that needed to be said was just hanging in the air around us.

"I didn't plan on coming back, you know," I said before taking another drink.

My drink was yanked from my hand, sat on the coffee table, and I was pinned to the couch before my brain could even process what had just happened. Damon's massive body hovered over me and he gripped my wrists in a tight grip above my head. The anger on his face was apparent as he forced himself between my legs and I bucked, trying to get him off.

"Either you were coming back on your own or I would make the choice for you."

I spit in his face. "You don't fucking own me, Damon."

He growled, using his free hand to wipe the spit from his face. "We will see about that."

Reaching down, he ripped at my jeans, forcing them down my legs as much as he could while I fought to get him off of me. He lifted just enough to flip me onto my stomach before pinning me down with his body. I heard his zipper as he undid his pants before he pulled my hips up to position himself at my entrance.

"Don't you fucking dare!" I screamed, thrashing even harder to free myself from his grasp.

He didn't give a shit and thrust into me. His massive size seemed to tear me in half as he thrust into me. Fuck.. A moan slipped from my lips as he pounded away, forcing his cock deep into my soaking cunt. I'd forgotten how good it felt for him to fill and stretch me to my limits. It didn't matter what my head wanted, my body had other plans. Bending to his will. I thrust my hips back to meet his as the pleasure in my core built. All that I could focus on was the sounds of flesh meeting flesh in rapid succession and our moans of pleasure filling the small room. I was so fucking close already.

He released my wrists and moved his hand to wrap around my throat from behind, cutting off my airway as he pulled me up so that my back was pressed firmly to his hard body.

His lips grazed my ear, the scruff of his beard moving along my skin as he whispered, "Come for me like a good little slut, Angel."

A shiver racked my body as he tightened his grip on my throat until I couldn't breathe and I fell over the edge. My orgasm ripped through me so hard that my vision blackened around the edges. He fucked me ruthlessly through the waves of pleasure that assaulted me until he was roaring out his own release. His cock pulsed inside of me, forcing my eyes to roll back.

He stayed inside of me, propped up on his elbows on either side of me as we lay there, catching our breath. He lightly kissed my shoulder and neck, forcing a breathy moan to escape my lips.

"You're mine, Angel, whether you like it or not." He whispers against my skin before getting up.

He left me lying there, a mixture of emotions filtering through my mind, as he redid his pants. From my position on the coach, I simply watched as he tossed an envelope on the kitchen counter. "From Jensen, he said it's to give him access to the mainframe once you're in."

He didn't look back at me or say another word as he walked out of the apartment, closing the door behind him. All I could do was lay there in a mix of pleasured bliss while my mind raced.

What the hell had I gotten myself into?

CHAPTER THIRTY-TWO

Angel

I'd started my old job at Hellfire again while we worked out all the details of the plan. The plan was a simple one. Make myself available to be snatched up. Since Dimitri had cut ties with the skin trade, there had been some backlash and girls kept going missing from the club. These guys wanted revenge against Dimitri and Damon. They wanted to cause them pain, so what better way than to snatch up their girls? They'd already tried it before, so it should be easy to do now. I'd even stopped wearing my knife since I didn't need to be killing these guys before they could take me to where Cherry was.

It had been about a week of Damon showing me off as his and working at the club again. I had to admit I'd missed him while I was away, but I wasn't stupid enough to tell him that. Every night I would leave on my own, hoping to attract the attention of the right people. If I wanted to be kidnapped, I had to look as helpless as possible. The fucks hadn't taken the bait, yet, so I was left floundering for what to do. None of this would work if they didn't take me.

I sat in the VIP lounge next to Damon as we had a meeting to discuss things. Dimitri had his laptop out on the coffee table where we could hear Jensen talking over the speakers. I needed as much information as possible for when I got access to the inside.

Dimitri had finally pulled his head out of his ass, though he still sported longer hair and a beard than normal. At least he was actively trying to get his girl back. He had spoken with the boss of the trade who his father had been working with. The fucker hadn't even hidden the fact that he'd taken Cherry and was housing her. He wouldn't tell us the details, but the meeting had gotten his head back in the game.

"So, we know who has her and where she is being held. That will make things much easier. I have sent over a blueprint of the estate where Lorenzo Russo does his business here in the states." Jensen spoke over the speakers and Damon pulled up the blueprints for me to go over.

"Depending on the guard situation and security, it shouldn't be too hard to get us out of there. Tell me more about this Lorenzo guy." I said, while looking through the blueprints on the screen.

More files popped up on the screen, including photos of the man. "Lorenzo, age 39, is the head of the Cosa Nostra. He took over a few years ago after the death of his father, Antonio. His primary organization takes place in Sicily, but he's been staying here in the states for a while now while he runs things remotely. He works in everything you'd expect from someone in the mafia, but drugs and human trafficking seem to be his biggest form of business. He worked with Madax to get his foot in the door here in the states which benefited him greatly. Fucking with him might not have been the best choice."

Looking over the files and photos, it was hard to miss the fact that the man was attractive. He had dark hair and deep brown eyes. He was everything you'd expect from an Italian mob boss, from the classy suits to the tattoos on his arms.

"Is Angel's tracker still working?" Damon asked from my side.

"Yes, sir. There have been no issues or delays in her tracker. We know where she's going and we can keep an eye on her. It tracks her location and vital signs. The envelope that was given to her holds a watch. Inside the face of which is a small drive she can insert into Lorenzo's personal computer. That should give me access to everything without him ever knowing. Just remember, it takes 30 seconds to connect. Make sure the time closes before removing it," Jensen said.

I forwarded all the information to my phone and sat back on the sofa with a sigh. "Thank you, Jensen. You've been a big help."

"My pleasure, Angel." He said before signing off.

"I hope you know what you're doing," Dimitri said, packing up his things to leave.

"I promise I'll get her back, Dimitri." I hoped he believed me. Even if I didn't get out, I was going to make sure Cherry was safe and back with him. The death of Madax was on me. I'd taken him out and fucked with Lorenzo's business. She had nothing to do with it.

He tilted his head in a slight nod before walking out, leaving just me and Damon in the room. He slipped his hand into mine, pulling me closer to him, where he forced me to face him, capturing the hair at the base of my head in a tight grip.

"You better come back too or I'll burn the fucking place down." He growled

I patted his chest lightly. "Hopefully it doesn't come to that, big guy."

He didn't waste a second as he captured my lips with his in a searing, hungry kiss. Gripping his shirt in my hand, I slipped onto his lap, straddling him. I didn't know what was going to happen once I was taken and if I never saw him again; I wanted to claim him, just like he'd claimed me.

He was already hard against my aching center as I ground myself along his impressive length. The man had no business being so fucking attractive and having such a massive dick. I was suddenly very happy that I'd picked out a skater-style dress to wear as his hands slid under the skirt to grip my hips. I made quick work unbuttoning his dress pants and freeing his dick, sliding his pocketknife from his pocket. He always had some array of weapons on his person, which was honestly really fucking hot. I sat the knife next to us on the couch as I slid my hands underneath the hem of his shirt. Filling his ab muscles tense underneath my palms.

"What do you plan to do with that, Angel?" Damon groaned against my lips as I took his dick in one of my hands, pumping him slowly.

"Let me worry about that." I lifted myself, sliding my panties to the side as I moved just the tip along my wet folds.

The small amount of friction made me moan softly. He let me tease us both for a moment before his grip on my hair tightened and he yanked my head to the side, giving him access to my neck. His lips trailed along my jaw and down my neck, biting and sucking, causing gasps to fall from my lips. I didn't know why, but I craved this man more than I'd craved anything else in my life. He'd worked his way under my skin and there was no getting rid of Damon Ashford once he sank his teeth into you. Maybe I had been an idiot to think I could just run off last time.

Positioning his cock at my entrance, I slowly slid down his length until he was fully sheathed. A deep groan left him from deep in his chest as his grip on my hips tightened, his teeth sinking into the tender flesh of my neck. I slowly began to ride him, sliding my soaking pussy almost completely up his dick before sliding back down. His head fell back against the couch as I rode him and he thrust his hips up to meet me, forcing him to hit that sweet spot deep within me. I took my time lazily unbuttoning his dress shirt to reveal the beautiful art that decorated his firm chest and abs. There was a small blank area right above his heart that would work perfectly for what I was about to do. I slowed my pace even further as I gripped the knife and flipped the blade open. I trailed it down his neck and over his nipples, being careful not to actually cut, as we continued our slow, tortuous pace. The groans and moans that left his lips had me clenching my cunt around his cock. Fuck, I loved the sounds this man-made when he was inside of me. Ever so slowly, I dragged the blade along that blank spot, letting the blade dig into his skin until a small drop of blood dripped down the surface. He groaned and I could have sworn he got even harder as he thrust into me harder.

"Be careful or you'll make me fuck it up." I tried to sound annoyed. Instead, it came out more like a breathy moan.

"Don't stop, Angel." He rasped.

I smiled as I worked the blade across his skin. Marking him just like he'd done to me. It was nice to know that he enjoyed receiving the pain just as much as he liked to dole it out. As I finished with the last letter, I leaned back slightly to admire my work. It simply read "Angel" in a crude sort of line work but I loved seeing the blood trail from the wound. I closed the knife, tossing it to the side as I leaned forward to run my tongue along the trail of blood. I moaned at the metallic taste and as soon as the sound of pleasure left my lips, Damon sprung to action. He gripped my hips forcibly as he flipped me over onto the couch and pistoned his hips even faster, driving his cock deeper into my waiting cunt. I wrapped my legs around his waist, thrusting my hips to match his thrusts, and slipped my hands into his hair, where I pulled him towards me into a searing kiss.

The kiss was just as rough as his hips, including a mix of teeth and tongue. He was devouring me in the best way, and all I wanted was more. More of this agonizing torture, more of this beautifully fucked up man who turned my world upside down. He reached down between us until his fingers found my swollen clit, where he rubbed me in slow circles without breaking the pace of his hips. The sensations had me arching my back and screaming his name as my orgasm ripped through me. He wasn't done though, and yanked me up into his arms. I gripped his shoulders to steady myself as he fucked up into me. Moving one of his hands to the front of my dress, he ripped the thin fabric down the center bearing my breasts. His mouth found my peaked nipple, and he sucked it into his mouth, biting down until I was sure he broke the skin, but I was too far gone to care as another orgasm built in the core of my stomach. I was almost certain that the first never stopped as another wave of pleasure washed over me. Damon was thorough as he worked me through my release, slowing his thrusts as I came down from the high. He released my nipple with an audible pop before running his tongue over the blood that beaded to the surface.

"I love it when you bleed for me, baby girl." He growled, thrusting his hips at a slow, hard pace.

He took the opposite nipple into his mouth, sucking gently and giving it the same attention as he had the other. His hands gripped my waist hard enough to leave bruises as he moved my hips to ride him as he thrust into me. It created the perfect amount of friction, and another orgasm built. His pure strength and drive had me aching all over again.

"Come for me again, Angel. I want every drop of your pleasure soaking my cock." He groaned deep in his throat, thrusting his hips faster. His body was tense, as if he was trying to hold himself back.

I used my hold on his shoulders to lift myself up and down his length to match his hard thrusts as my body trembled. A whimper escaped my lips as a third orgasm shot through me and he soon followed after, filling me with his come.

We were a mess as he leaned back onto the sofa, never slipping out of me. I rested my head on his shoulder as we both tried to catch our breath and admired the new mark I'd given him. The blood had begun to dry by this point, so I lightly traced my finger along the outline of the lettering. Damon's arm snaked around me, holding me close to him, and his chin rested on the top of my head.

We stayed like this for some time. Just wrapped in the other's arms and a comforting silence. I was spent, and I felt safe in his arms. I wasn't sure if I would ever be able to feel like this again, so I savored every moment. A deep-seated pity filled me the longer we stayed like this. The calm before the storm.

CHAPTER THIRTY-THREE

Damon

Sitting here with Angel wrapped in my arms was like my own personal heaven. Her soft curves fit perfectly against mine and I didn't want the moment to end. I knew Angel wasn't the lovey-dovey type, and I highly doubted I'd ever get her to admit she cared about me, but she'd just marked me. She'd carved her name above my heart and staked her claim on me. Just thinking about the way she had cut into me had me growing hard inside of her again. A man could die happily buried balls deep in her warm, wet cunt.

I rested my chin on the top of her head as she curled into me. Her sweet lavender and lilac scent surrounded me. I'd fucking missed her, and I was pissed that I could lose her again. She was putting herself in danger, trying to get Cherry back. It was a good plan, but I still didn't like it. I meant what I had said. If she didn't come back, I'd go in there, guns blazing and burn the fucking place to the ground.

We stayed like this, enjoying our time together. It was nice to hold her like this. It was almost like back at the beginning, when we would spend the entire night fucking only to fall asleep in each other's arms. I wasn't sure how I was such a lucky bastard that she'd picked me to spend her time with. While she was gone, I didn't know what to do with myself. I had just spent the time stalking her every move until she had settled down.

It was almost closing time, so we got ourselves situated back into our clothes. I smiled to myself as Angel groaned when she noticed there was no fixing her dress. I hadn't meant to rip it, but her frustration afterward was well worth it.

"You owe me a new damn dress." She seethed, tying the loose sides into a knot.

It wasn't perfect, but it would be good enough for getting her home tonight without everyone on staff seeing her tits. I walked over to her, grabbed her hips to pull her flush against me, and placed light kisses along her jaw.

"You can have whatever you want, Angel. All you have to do is ask."

She huffed, rolling her eyes, and headed towards the door. Before she could make it out, I gave her plump little ass a good slap. I couldn't get enough of her.

Walking into work, I was surprised to see Dimitri sitting at the bar with a drink so early in the day. Worry ate at my gut as I made my way over and Zack just slid a tumbler of scotch in front of me. Yep, not good.

"Just spit it out," I growled, glaring at them both.

"They grabbed Angel last night," Zack said, looking over at me with worry. He pushed his phone towards me on the bar top. The video of a white van pulling up and snatching my girl was on full display.

My vision tunneled as I threw back the shot that had been offered and stormed out of the bar. I knew this had been Angel's plan, but that didn't mean I had to be happy about it. Fuck this bullshit.

CHAPTER THIRTY-FOUR

Angel

Fuck, my head was pounding. I didn't want to open my eyes, and I felt like I'd been run over by a fucking mack truck. Groaning, I rolled over and realized I was lying on a hard mattress that reeked of human filth and mold. Or maybe that was just wherever I was.

Toto, we weren't in Kansas anymore. I opened my eyes to a dark room where it was impossible to make much out. All I could tell was that the space was dark and moldy. Wiping my hands down my face, I noticed my hands were in chains, like you'd see in those pirate movies where they wrapped around your wrists and ankles. Great. Chained up in a dark hole. I fucking hated being chained up, but that could only mean that those bastards had finally taken the bait and snatched me up.

My brain was foggy, and I couldn't remember anything after leaving the club last night. With the way my head felt and the nausea, I was sure they'd used some sort of drug to knock me out. All I could do now was wait and see how things played out.

I plopped back onto the mattress that was laid on the floor and made myself as comfortable as possible while I waited for my captors to show themselves.

I awoke with a start to the sound of a door being swung open and hitting the wall. Jumping up, I stood to face who had barged into the room. I might be chained to the wall, but like hell, if I wouldn't put up a fight. All I could see was the silhouette of a man as he entered the room. He was big and in casual clothes, from the looks of it.

"Boss wants to see you." He said in a gravelly, heavily accented voice.

Seeing the boss was probably the best way to find my way to Cherry and get us both out of here. I allowed the man to unlock my chain from the wall and followed him out of the room. It was fucking bright outside of that room. The fluorescent lights lead up a flight of stairs.

Glancing around, I noticed a handful of other doors like the one I'd just walked out off. Did they really leave people in those dark holes?

Getting a good look at the man escorting me, I took in his appearance as we made our way up the stairs to a main floor that was decorated in white and grey finery. He was most likely in his late forties, with wrinkles beginning to appear on his face. He was obviously Sicilian, with tattoos on his arms, salt, and pepper hair slicked back, and a matching short beard. His brown eyes scanned the area as we walked, and he carried himself with an air of caution and confidence. Dressed in a black button-up shirt with the sleeve rolled up and a brown vest overtop. He kept the rest of his outfit casual, with a pair of tailored blue jeans and dress casual shoes. He didn't speak much, and I took the time as we walked to take in my surroundings.

The floors were made of pale grey hardwood. From the looks and feel of it, it was real hardwood as my bare feet padded quietly over the smooth surface. All the walls were a pale cream color and were decorated with beautiful monochromatic artwork. The pieces were mostly abstract, but upon closer inspection, they depicted nude men and women in erotic scenes. The place screamed money and elegance without being over the top. There were a few windows, but it appeared as if they were all sealed shut. I guess you couldn't be too careful when you kidnapped people. That took slipping through an open window out of the escape plan. I'd have to find a way for us to get out.

The man stopped at a set of grey double doors and pushed one open, letting me go in first. Walking into the room, I found an office with wall-to-wall bookshelves up the high ceiling. A modern desk sat in the middle. The top was stained dark grey and was held up by golden legs in the shape of rectangles on each side. Behind the desk, I could see a set of floor-to-ceiling curtains that were pulled closed. The chair that went with it was a dark grey wingback office chair, and my eyes snagged on the man sitting there.

He was typing away on his laptop with the screen illuminating his black-framed glasses. He was nicely tanned, showing off that he spent his time in the sun. His beard was well-groomed, fading into his dark hair. Said hair was short on the sides and long at the top, which was slicked back, and meticulously styled. His face was angular, with a straight nose that complimented the rest of his face. He was dressed in a black three-piece suit, and black leather oxford shoes, and his black and silver striped tie was loose around his neck. This man was the one and only Lorenzo Russo. The pictures that Jensen had sent didn't do this man justice. If he'd been anyone else, I'd call him attractive, but his line of work lessened the effect.

As I stopped in front of his desk with my escort behind me, I jiggled the chains on my wrists to get his attention. Have I mentioned how much I hate being chained up?

"Are these really necessary?" I asked, hoping one of these idiots would get the hint and take them off.

Lorenzo looked up from his computer screen, eyeing me from my bare feet up to my face. "I've heard that I should not underestimate you, Angel."

His Italian accent was thick, and the deep tenor was absolutely yummy. It flowed over my skin, breaking me out in goosebumps. Why were the most attractive men always the most disgusting? It would make things easier if they were fat and ugly.

"So, you know who I am?" I said, letting my arms fall in front of me. Maybe if I didn't seem like a threat, they wouldn't keep me chained up.

"I know everything about you." He stood from his chair, took his glasses off, placed them on the desk, and walked around the desk to stand in front of me. He was fucking tall, taller than Damon, and if I had to guess, he was 6'4". "Angel Hart, 28. You had a younger sister who was murdered 8 years ago. Then you took your time killing the men responsible, including my late partner Madax Ashford. You're intimate with Damon Ashford and you just got back after you had settled into a small town in North Carolina. If I were a betting man, I would assume that is due to my men taking Ms. Vahn. Am I correct?"

I glared up at him. I wouldn't give him the satisfaction of any other response. With him standing this close, I could smell his sandalwood and patchouli scent. It was a warm, comforting scent that only made me dislike him more. I wasn't sure what the best way to play this was. He obviously knew me and the things I'd done. I was a threat and a wild card. He wouldn't just let me roam and find a way out. His chocolate eyes studied me, watching my every move. He was smart, and he wouldn't be easy to fool like I'd been hoping. Fuck, what had I gotten myself into?

"So, where is Cherry?" I said, keeping my voice as calm as possible.

"She is up in a room." He sounded so matter-of-fact about that statement as he leaned against the desk, putting himself closer to my eye level. "Don't worry. She's safe and remains untouched. I only took her to prove a point to those boys that took over my late partner's affairs."

I felt my shoulders relax, knowing that nothing bad had happened to her, but I was still cautious. They obviously took us for a reason. I needed to know what he was planning. "Then what the hell do you want with us?"

"Like I said, to prove a point."

"Which would be?" He smiled at my question.

That smile was dangerous and wicked. The man was fucking charming. I'd give him that. I really didn't expect him to grab my chains and pull me flush against him. Holding me between his legs as he got in my face.

"I'm sure you'd love to know, *principessa.*" He gripped my chin, using his thumb to pull down on my bottom lip. "*Hai una bocca così bella, Angel.*"

I snapped my teeth at his finger, just missing, and he pulled his hand away from my face. This fucker was going to piss me off. It made me even madder that I didn't know what the fuck he was saying. Based on the look on his face and body language, I was sure it had been suggestive in some way.

Despite my inappropriate behavior, he simply smiled at me before speaking to the other guy. "Dante…" He spoke followed by a string of Italian I had no chance in hell understanding. At least now I knew the guy's name was Dante. That much I could understand. Lorenzo pushed me back lightly so that he was standing in front of me and handed my chains to Dante. He took the chains and led me out of the room. We went up 2 flights of stairs and to the door of what I assumed was a bedroom. The grey door locked from the outside with a pin pad and I watched as Dante typed in the numbers to unlock the door. 1-3-6-8-4-2. He pushed me into the room and I staggered in. Those numbers probably wouldn't help me much, but I'd much rather be safe than sorry later on.

"Angel!"

Glancing up at my name being called, I found Cherry rushing towards me, but she stopped short as Dante stepped into the room. He made quick work of undoing my restraints before stepping back towards the door.

He glared at me, throwing the chains over his shoulder. "Don't try anything stupid. Bathroom and closet are through those doors."

I looked to where he'd pointed to see the two grey doors as he shut and locked the door. Cherry threw her arms around me, and on instinct, I hugged her back.

"Why are you here, Angel?" She asked as she roamed her eyes over me as if searching for injury while I did the same to her.

"I came to get you out. Are you okay? Have they touched you? I'm going to strangle those assholes with their intestines." She took my hand and led me over to the far side of the room where two twin-sized beds with a nightstand between them sat. She sat me on the unmade bed and took my hands in hers as she told me all that had happened.

"So they snatched me at the club a few weeks ago while I was leaving work. I woke up in a dark room in the basement before they brought me up here. I'm fine, and no one has done anything. Lorenzo is the guy that worked with Madax, but I don't think he plans on selling us. He's just trying to get back at Dimitri for ending their business agreements. I don't know much, other than Lorenzo is the guy in charge of the girls that go missing from the club. He's bad news though, and I get a really bad feeling from him."

"So, have they just been leaving you locked in here?" I asked, while looking around the room. The place was bare besides the beds with white linens, the grey nightstand with a lamp on top, and the doors that led to the closet and bathroom on the opposite wall.

"Pretty much. They bring me books and puzzles to keep me busy and food throughout the day." She glanced out of the window. "It's getting late, so they should bring dinner soon."

I got up and walked over to the window. Of course, it was sealed shut like the others. If I stayed locked up in this room, how was I going to get us out of here?

CHAPTER THIRTY-FIVE

Damon

"Do you fucking know where she is?" I growled into the phone.

"Yes, she's at the estate and from the looks of it, she's been in the same room of the estate for the past week." Jensen's voice said over the speaker. It had been a week since they'd taken Angel and I wasn't handling things well.

What if she couldn't find her way out? Who knew what that fucker was doing to her? Since the news broke, I'd been dragging people into my basement. I was on edge and was ready to storm that damn building to get my girl back. This had been Angel's plan, but I didn't give a shit. I couldn't handle not knowing if she was okay.

"You have to trust she knows what she's doing," Dimitri said from his seat in front of my desk. He'd been oddly calm about all of this.

I shot a glare at him before looking back at the screen to see the blinking red dot. That was Angel. She was alive and being kept in that room. What the fuck was taking her so long to get them out of there?

"I received an invitation for us. Lorenzo is having an *event* at the estate this weekend. Maybe we will see the girls then." Dimitri said, taking a drink from his tumbler. His drinking was the only sign that something was wrong with him. He was just as stressed about the situation as I was, but he was the only person I could be mad at right now.

"I'll keep an eye on her tracker, sir. I will let you know if anything changes." Jensen said, the sound of keys typing away in the background heard over the speaker on my phone.

I didn't say anything as I hung up the phone. I was over this bullshit.

"Stop screaming like a little bitch." I growled at the man dangling from the ceiling of my basement.

He was just some low-life druggy who hadn't paid us a debt he owed. He probably didn't deserve all this, but I was in a mood. I couldn't hurt Angel. Damon had kicked me out of his office during my last meeting with him, and so fucking up this low life was the only thing I could do to keep myself calm.

He screamed as I sliced through his skin, peeling the flesh from the muscle. It was fun watching how much a human body could handle while you slowly skinned them alive. I tossed the flesh into a nearby bucket and poured a handful of salt into my palm.

"You owe us an enormous debt, Johnny. Got anything you can give to make us even?" I asked, watching the snot and tears run down the fuck's face.

Not such a big man when you were about to be food for the worms. He sniffled, screamed, and begged. There was nothing he could offer us. He was a waste of oxygen. Why Madax had kept him around and funded his addictions, I'd never understand.

The list of idiots I needed to dispose of was extensive, but they at least kept me busy. I rubbed the salt into his fresh wound and thrived on the screams of agony. Inflicting pain always made my dick hard, and I was to the point of bursting from the adrenaline pumping through my veins.

I took my time skinning the fucker until he passed out from the blood loss and pain. He'd bleed out within about five minutes. I'd been skinning him for hours. Never letting his body heal or be able to stop the blood from flowing. So I left him hanging there while I made my way to the basement shower. Before the water would warm up, I stripped out of my jeans and climbed into the shower. I let the cold water wash over me, plastering my hair to my face, neck, and back. I just stood there watching the red-stained water run down the drain.

I felt lost without her. Like a rabid beast was clawing under my skin to get out. I'd just gotten her back. She'd made progress and claimed me. How could she just be taken right after that? The thought of her in that place with my enemies was leaving me strung tight, about to break.

I'd get my girl back if it was the last thing I ever did.

CHAPTER THIRTY-SIX

Angel

Things went by slowly. Cherry and I stayed locked in this room together. We talked and caught up about life since I'd left, played board games, put together puzzles, and did anything to keep ourselves busy. I was fucking bored and found myself agitated as the week went on.

A week. I'd been locked in this fucking room for a week. The only people I saw were Cherry and Dante when he brought us our meals. I was so over this bullshit. I didn't get how she'd been able to stand it and stay her usual bubbly self. Granted, she wasn't happy, but she was handling things so well. I knew things could be much worse for us, but I still couldn't stand being a prisoner. We had a closet full of clothes and shoes with a fully stocked bathroom. Overall, we were fed and taken care of.

As of now, Cherry was sitting on her bed putting together a 500-piece puzzle and I was lying on mine reading some sort of rom-com, contemporary romance that she'd recommended. It was the story of some literary agent who goes off to a small town and falls in love with an editor she's had a grudge against. It's a good read and I find myself lost in the story. I wouldn't have picked it for myself.

Romance isn't my thing, if my *relationship* with Damon is any indication. When did I even start referring to it as a relationship? There must be something in the fucking water here because I'm not into all that romance shit. I guess I miss the brute, though. We'd had a good thing last time I was in town and things had picked up again fairly quickly as soon as I walked back through the doors of Hellfire. I really needed to get out of here if that was the way my brain was working.

A knock came at the door before Dante walked in. He was dressed in his usual style of blue jeans, a pair of loafers, and had on a white button-up dress shirt. I'd come to learn that while he dressed nicely, he also liked a bit of casual comfort. He didn't speak to us much outside of making sure we didn't need anything. He walked over to my side of the bed and that's when I noticed the handcuffs in his hand. I guess the plus side was that it was just a standard pair of cuffs.

"*Il Capo*, would like to speak with you, Ms. Hart." He said, holding his hand out for me to take. They switched between Italian and English, so it didn't take me long to pick up that il capo meant *the boss*. I still couldn't understand the shit Dante said sometimes, but I at least got it.

I eyed the cuffs in his hand while placing my book face down on the bed. "Are those really necessary?"

"*Sì.*"

A man of few words. I rolled my eyes before throwing my legs over the side of the bed and standing in front of him. I held my wrists out as he secured the cuffs before walking out the door. Cherry was quiet as he escorted me out of the room and locked the door behind us.

He led me back downstairs to the same office as before. I took note of every turn and even noticed the front entryway was unguarded. Maybe that could be our way out. Yeah, going out the front door probably wasn't the best choice, but it was the only option I'd seen since we'd been here. I'd need to see more of the place if I was going to figure out a way to get Cherry out of here, hopefully getting myself out too.

Like before, he opened the door to the office and motioned for me to go in first. The only difference this time was that the large window behind the desk had the curtains drawn, allowing the bright sunshine to fill the space. I walked directly up to the desk, my hands bound in front of me, and glared at the man sitting there on his computer. Lorenzo glanced up at me and smiled that charming smile of his.

"Angel, I'm glad you could come to speak with me." He trailed his eyes over my body. I'd been in a pair of black Soffe shorts and a white tank top and I hadn't bothered to change for this.

"I didn't realize I had a choice." I presented my bound hands with a classic eye roll. This dude really got on my nerves.

Lorenzo stood and walked around the desk to stand in front of me again. He grabbed hold of my chin, forcing me to look up into his warm, chocolate eyes, "*Dante, dacci un po' di privacy.*"

Maybe figuring out some of what they said wouldn't be too hard. All I understood the words were meant for Dante and based on privacy; he was telling him to leave just us in this room. While Dante slipped out of the office, I didn't take my eyes off Lorenzo as I glared up at him. What the hell did this fucker want?

"You are absolutely stunning, *principessa*." He said, trailing that thumb over my bottom lip again.

His free hand gripped my bound wrists, and the hand slid from my face as he reached into his pocket, extracting a key. He didn't waste a second as he unlocked my cuffs and dropped them and the key on the desk.

"I am trusting you not to do anything rash, *principessa*." He said, walking back to sit in his chair.

I stood there and rubbed my wrists while watching his every move. I didn't understand the point of all this. Was he trying to gain my trust or play some sort of fucked up game?

"What do you want, Lorenzo?" I asked.

He simply smiled, folding his hands under his chin as he leaned forward on the desk. "Please call me Enzo."

"Whatever. What do you want, *Enzo*?" I growled out between clenched teeth.

His eyes seemed to shine as he looked me over, his gaze lingering on my lips. "There are a few things I want."

"Care to elaborate? Or is this going to be a pointless conversation?"

"I would like to have my old partnership back with Ashford Enterprise. I would also like to have you." He said all of this matter of factually while I just stood there contemplating his words. There was no way Dimitri would start up a partnership with him. He hated the skin trade and made it his mission to get rid of that part of the business when Madax was out of the picture. He would do anything to get Cherry back, though, even cutting a deal with Lorenzo if he needed. I was sure I could play this in my favor and find some way to screw over this asshole standing in front of me.

"The only way you're getting that deal back is if you give Cherry back to Dimitri. Until then, he won't be interested in striking any sort of deal with you." I purposely didn't mention the fact that he'd just admitted that he wanted me, as if I were some piece of property meant to be bought and sold. The thought had my blood boiling. This guy was a fucking monster.

"Fair point. This weekend, I am hosting an event here at my home. I have taken the liberty of inviting Mr. Ashford and his brother. Ms. Vahn is free to leave with them that evening on one condition." His smile turned almost mocking.

"What condition?" I already knew what he would say.

"He will sign a legal contract with me that night and you stay here with me, under full watch, of course. You will be free to do as you please, so long as you remain here on the grounds, *principessa.*" His expression was smug now as he watched me shift my weight uncomfortably.

"Deal, but I'm sure you'll be disappointed." I crossed my arms over my chest, glancing over at the books that lined the walls.

"We shall see."

CHAPTER THIRTY-SEVEN

Angel

The weekend came quickly and in the late afternoon, a parade of people came into the room to get us ready for whatever event they were having. They got to work on Cherry first. They left her short blonde hair down in elegant waves and applied a light layer of makeup that didn't cover up her natural, innocent beauty. She looked stunning as they led her into our walk-in closet to find the perfect dress and shoes for the evening.

I hadn't told her yet that she'd be going home tonight while I stayed behind. I'd thought out a plan that could work in everyone's favor. For now, though, I needed to focus on my end of the bargain I had struck with Lorenzo. Things could get messy if everything didn't go exactly right.

An older woman in her fifties got to work on my hair and makeup. She didn't speak outside of asking for my opinion on looks. I obviously only had one request, a bold red lipstick. I needed the confidence boost if I was going to play my part tonight.

Lorenzo hadn't given me details of what the event actually was, but I was unaware I'd be showing up on his arm. I had been instructed to do everything he asked without question and to enjoy myself. Most of all, I couldn't make a scene or he wouldn't let Cherry leave. Every instinct was telling me to stab him in the gut, but I couldn't force a slave life on the closest person I'd had to being an actual friend. She needed to get back to Dimitri and Zack. I'd figure out how to get myself out of this situation.

Hopefully.

When the woman was finished with my hair and makeup, I looked into the mirror to see a silver smokey eye that made my blue eyes appear even bluer. She'd used black eyeliner to create a winged cat eye effect, giving the perfect siren eye look. The face makeup was light to appear natural and the red lipstick was fairly close to my go-to shade. I could already tell it was just regular lipstick and not a stain like I was used to. I'd have to be careful not to have this one streaked across my face. The older lady had even left the lipstick for me on the nightstand in case I'd need to reapply it. My hair was placed up into a low, elegant bun at the base of my neck, with curled pieces of midnight hair framing my face.

By the time the woman was satisfied with how I looked, Cherry was walking out of the closet in a mid-calf length dress. It was pale blue, and the fabric held a light shimmer to it. It fitted to her frame with a slight flare at the hips, with a cottage core short sleeve neckline. She'd paired it with a pair of silver strappy heels. With her, they were definitely going for a light, innocent look. It suited her and her personality, and I was glad she was going to get out of this situation. If she didn't get out now, Lorenzo wouldn't keep treating us so well. I didn't want her to face the dark side of what Lorenzo was a part of. It would break her. I could handle it all on my own if it meant she got out tonight.

I assured the women fussing over us I could pick my dress as I made my way into the closet. I lightly ran my hand over the array of colorful dresses. Like hell, if I was going to be wearing something so colorful tonight. No, bright wasn't my style. I went to the drawers that housed underwear and picked out a black lace bra and thong set, slipping them on. The lace bra held my breasts up, giving me a fuller look than I actually had.

I took my time going through the dresses until I found the perfect one in black. It was floor length with a flared shirt and a slit up to the mid-thigh. The bodice was draped in lace and the v-neck dipped down between my breasts to show off a good amount of cleavage, showcasing the floral and moon sternum tattoo I'd gotten as soon as I ended up in my new life. Its long, lace sleeves fell to the back of my hands in the shape of a V and the see-through material showed off the ink on my arms. To finish the look, I added a pair of black strappy heels.

When the woman finally left the room, I sat down on the bed next to Cherry, taking her hand in mine as I slipped her a piece of paper. "Cherry, you're getting out of here tonight and leaving with Dimitri. I need you to give this note to him and Damon."

"What about you?" She nearly screeched at me. I fought the urge to cover her mouth, afraid someone could be listening.

"I'll find another way out. Tonight, when you see Dimitri, I need you to give him this note immediately. You're getting out of here depends on it. He has to do things exactly what this note says or we are all fucked." I gripped her hands tightly, hoping that she'd do as I asked without complaint, "No matter what, make sure Dimitri and Damon do as the note says. I'm not sure what will happen if they don't."

I didn't like keeping things from her. I knew exactly what would happen to us both if the boys didn't do what needed to be done. We'd be just another set of girls who went missing and are then sold off to some sick old fuck, or worse. She nodded, tears filling her eyes as she took the note and slipped it into the top of her dress. Tonight was going to be a long night.

CHAPTER THIRTY-EIGHT

Angel

I was feeling anxious as Dante escorted us down to the event. From the sound of things, there was already a large crowd behind the double doors. This was a new area of the house, so I kept an eye out for where the guards were and any exits. I couldn't be too careful. Regardless of what transpired here tonight, Cherry was going home. I'd kill whoever I had to in order to make that happen.

Lorenzo was standing at the double doors, speaking to the guards off to the side, when he noticed us approaching. He greeted Dante with a slight nod before turning to Cherry.

"You look absolutely radiant, Ms. Vahn." He said, kissing the back of her hand. She was quick to pull her hand free and take a step back from him..

Dante presented her with his arm as he led her through the doors as Lorenzo made his way to me. Even in these tall ass heels, I had to look up at him as he stood in front of me. He gripped my waist, pulling me flush against him. His sandalwood and patchouli scent surrounded me as he placed a light kiss on my cheek.

He whispered against my skin in Italian, trailing his free hand up my throat to my chin.

"You realize I have no clue what the fuck you're saying." Even I sounded snarky to my own ears, but it only seemed to delight him as he flashed that charming smile.

"You will learn, *principessa*. Now watch your tone and behave this evening." He offered me his arm. I slipped my hand onto his arm as he escorted me inside. Even though all I wanted to do was slam the heel of these stupid shoes into his eye socket.

The place was packed, and I was shocked at what was before me. I had been expecting something similar to what Madax had taken me to the last time I was at an *event*, but this was something completely different. The area was covered in plush couches and there was sex equipment spread out around the room. There was a mix of nude bodies, men in suits, and women in fabulous gowns, watching others in an array of positions. It was an orgy, a sex dungeon placed into the middle of an extravagant ballroom.

I was sure my jaw would have ended up on the floor if I hadn't been so tense. Scanning the room, my eyes caught on Cherry standing next to Dimitri in a corner, but my eyes immediately zeroed in on the brute of a man standing next to them. Damon. His long hair was tied up in a sleek bun at the base of his neck, his beard looking a bit more grown out than the last time I'd seen him. He was dressed in an all-black suit with a deep red tie. His eyes were already on me as Lorenzo led me through the crowd. Even from this distance, I could tell he hadn't been sleeping well with the dark circles under his eyes. Every bone in my body was screaming at me to run to him. To the safety and comfort, he provided me. My heart felt like it was in a vise.

"Don't worry, *principessa*. You'll get to speak with him soon enough." Lorenzo whispered in my ear.

I tore my eyes away from Damon to look at Lorenzo. I didn't like the way he said that. It was as if there was a hidden meaning behind it. With him, it wouldn't surprise me. I glanced back at Damon as Lorenzo led me to one scene at the far end of the room.

On a platform there was a woman tied to a St. Andrew's Cross and a man in tight leather pants and a mask was whipping her with a cat-o'-nine-tails. Looking closely, I noticed a glazed look over the girl's eyes. She was drugged. Her moans filled the air every time she was struck. I didn't know if it was self-inflicted or if she'd just been given the drugs to be easier to control, but considering the shit, I knew Lorenzo was a part of I'd have to go with the latter.

We made our way around the room, Lorenzo speaking to people here and there as he showed me all the different scenes going on. It would have been hot if the people weren't being forced into their performances. The last scene we came across was of a woman being railed by two men. It appeared as if they were all into it, even though each participant shared that glazed look as they fucked each other.

"Do you like what you see, *principessa*?" Lorenzo asked as he stood behind me, rubbing my arms lightly.

"What I see are a bunch of drugged sex slaves who are being forced into a shitty lifestyle." I didn't care if it pissed him off. Honestly, I wanted to make him regret wanting to keep me.

My sass didn't seem to faze him as he chuckled, grabbed my hand, and led me out of the room. It was so quiet out in the hall in comparison. "Where are you taking me?"

He didn't answer me until he led me into a separate room. The walls were painted a deep red and the four-poster bed was covered in black silk with tulle drapery. Along the walls were drawers and everything you'd expect to be in a sex room hung along the walls. Walking around, I ran my hand lightly over floggers, whips, and many other things. I had no clue what they were used for. I heard the door clicking shut before Lorenzo made his way over to me.

"Why bring me here? You've made it clear that if I *misbehave*, you won't let Cherry leave." I looked everywhere but at him as I made my way around the room.

"Because I have a surprise for you, *principessa*." A knock sounded at the door. "Ah, and there it is. Come in."

For the millionth time, it felt like tonight I was shocked to see Damon enter the room. What the fuck was he doing here? I glanced over at Lorenzo, who simply smiled as he took off his suit jacket and loosened his tie.

He took a seat on one of the chairs facing the bed before he elaborated, "You're mine now, *principessa*. I thought it would be nice for you to have one last parting moment with your lover."

Looking at Damon, he seemed just as surprised as I was. He didn't take his eyes off me, though. It was as if he were trying to memorize every single feature of me. The way his gaze heated as he looked over my body. That warm feeling I always got from his stares washed over me. God, I had missed him this past week. I looked back at Lorenzo with a glare.

"What's the fucking catch, *Enzo?*" I was pissed off and seething.

He ignored me as he focused on Damon. "Has your brother agreed to the deal?"

"Yes," was Damon's gruff reply. His deep voice sent goosebumps over my skin. I was cold and heated all at the same time.

Lorenzo smiled and motioned towards the bed. Damon looked between me and it. He was just as unsure about all of this as I was, apparently. I kept my glare trained on Lorenzo. The charming smile hadn't left his face. I'd never wanted to hurt someone simply to cause them pain as I did that man.

He finally decided to answer me, "I'd like to watch, *principessa*, maybe join if I am so inclined. Pretend like I'm not even here."

Damon shut the door and finally walked over to me, his hand slipping around the back of my neck to pull me close to him. I sighed as his sweet mahogany scent enveloped me and I melted into his touch. I wasn't sure about all this, but damn if I was going to give up my possible last chance of being with him. His other hand gripped my waist as our bodies molded together. His thumb worked for slow, soothing circles on my hip.

"Hello, Angel." He growled through his teeth so that only I could hear. I couldn't get a read on him, which bothered me. Usually, I could read him so easily, and use his mood to my advantage, but it was as if I were seeing him now for the first and final time.

"Damon," I meant to sound more confident, but his name tumbled from my lips like a prayer. I hoped that Cherry had given them my note. That Damon had read the part specifically for him. It would have explained everything. I didn't want Damon to think I was doing this to get away from him again. The short distance had made me realize just how wrong I'd been to leave him behind.

CHAPTER THIRTY-NINE

Damon

Dimitri, Zack, and I had just arrived at the *party* Lorenzo was throwing. It wasn't our first time at one of his events, so we knew we'd be walking into a sexcapade. The place was full and there were different scenes going on around the room. People were placing bids on those participating in scenes. Where the old fuck had done auctions, Lorenzo did things a bit differently. He wanted to show off the skills of the people he was selling.

Dimitri was tense next to me as he scanned the area. He was sure we'd walk in to find Cherry forced into one of the scenes and drugged like the others. He gave an audible sigh of relief when it was clear she wasn't being sold or on one of the stages around the room.

"Thank goodness she isn't being forced into this mess." Zack said from next to me.

Looking at him, his eyes had snagged on a little redhead who was strapped to a cross being whipped. From the look of pity on his face, I knew the kid was about to do something stupid. But I had more to worry about than what he was thinking. We stood off to the side, watching as the night began. My eyes swept the floor for any sign of my girl. Still nothing. Lorenzo wasn't even in attendance, so things hadn't really gotten started.
"Fuck," I glanced at Dimitri to see his eyes wide, staring off to the far side of the room.

Following his gaze, I understood what had caught his attention. Cherry was being escorted in on the arm of Lorenzo's men. They were heading straight for us. Cherry's face lit up as they approached and once she was close enough, she leaped into my brother's arms. He looked her over frantically, asking if she was okay, which she reassured him she was. The guy, Dante, I believe his name was, just walked off. That was either a very good or very bad sign. Once hellos had been exchanged between everyone, Cherry handed a note to Dimitri.

"Angel said that you two needed to read it. She said it was important and couldn't wait."

Dimitri opened the note, but I couldn't pay any mind as Angel walked into the room on Lorenzo's arm. Yeah, that note was definitely bad fucking news. At least for me, anyway. My gut was rarely wrong. As soon as my girl was in the room, her eyes took in everything. She'd always been the type to scope out a situation, and she knew where everything was in a room. Her eyes stopped roaming as she looked directly at me. The fire that always consumed me when she was around fired up again. For the first time since she'd been taken, I felt fucking alive.

She was dressed in a sexy as hell black gown, and I couldn't help but want to tear it off of her delicate skin. I watched as she stayed on Lorenzo's arm and he escorted her around the room. Every now and then, he would whisper something to her to grab her attention. Her gaze always found its way back to me.

"Damon, this isn't good." Dimitri said, handing me the note.

Glancing his way, I noticed that Zack wasn't with us anymore as I took the note. Reading over it, I wanted to crumple it up and kill something.

Dimitri, I cut a deal to get Cherry out. Lorenzo wants to start up a new contract with you. The same one that Madax had with him. In exchange, he's willing to let Cherry go. Don't worry, she's been safe and taken care of.

I'm not sure what he'd originally planned, but things must have changed when they took me. Part of the deal was that she could go, but I had to stay. Just do what he asks of you. It won't stick. I have a plan. Keep in contact with Jensen. I'll send him everything I can to take this fucker down. Damon, remember what you said to me. Make it a promise. I only ask that you give me some time to get as much information as I can. A month tops. Just in case things don't work out like I want, make sure you take them all out.

I know this is shitty to do this way. I should have said it sooner, but I'm yours, Damon, and always will be.

-Angel

Now I was fucking pissed. She would never say that shit to me. I knew her. She wasn't the romantic type and if she was saying this in a letter; she wasn't planning on making it out of here. My blood boiled as I crumpled up the letter and handed it back to Dimitri.

CHAPTER FORTY

Angel

"You're mine, Angel," Damon whispered so that only I could hear it.

I almost melted at that. He'd gotten my letter. Shit, he'd gotten my letter. I'd admitted my feelings for him in a fucking letter. What the fuck had I been thinking? I couldn't take it back now, and this was going to be my last moment with him.

"Yours," As the word left my lips, he crashed his lips to mine.

The world faded to just us as I focused on Damon. He forced his tongue into my mouth, using his hand in my hair to angle me exactly how he wanted. His hungry kiss consumed me and I slipped my fingers into his hair, pulling him closer to me as he devoured me. This kiss

263

was hot and desperate, and I couldn't get him close enough. My hands slipped down his shoulder to his chest, where I wasted no time at all working my way through his buttons. My hands roamed his bare chest as his lips trailed down my chin and neck, biting and sucking on my skin. I moaned his name. He knew exactly what to do with my body to make me tick.

"Damon, why don't you get undressed and lie on the bed?"

My eyes shot to Lorenzo. What the fuck happened to pretending he wasn't here? Now he was going to order us around like his little fucking playthings. I wanted to stab him in his fucking face. Damon's hands tightened on me as he straightened, glaring at Lorenzo just like I was. He wasn't the type to be bossed around, and I could see the rage shimmering in his crystal blue eyes.

Pressing my lips to his bare chest, I whispered, "Just do what he says. I'm not sure how to play all this in our favor, but until Cherry is out of here, you have to listen to him."

I felt his body relax to my touch before he stepped away just enough to undress. Without taking his eyes off me, he loosened his tie enough to slip over his head, tossing it over onto a nearby sex bench. I really hoped the shit in here had been cleaned. Next to go was his suit jacket and shirt. His muscles rippled as he moved, showing off all the ink that I loved and the healing wound where I'd carved my name into his chest.. I couldn't keep my hands off him as I ran my fingers along the jagged lines of my name over his heart. It was healing nicely, considering it had only been a week. Damon removed his belt, sliding it through the loops of his pants, then tossing it over with the rest of his clothes. I lightly kissed where I'd marked him as I replaced his hands with mine to unbutton his pants, sliding them and his boxers down his toned ass and thighs. As I pushed them down farther, I trailed my lips down his body. He adjusted his stance as he slipped his shoes off and then stepped out of his pants for me. The tattoos covering this man's body always had me feeling feral. I wanted to trace every single one with my tongue. To trail my lips and tongue up his thighs to his hard cock. I might be overly responsive to him, but I was sure by now that the feelings were mutual.

I slid my tongue up the underside of his length, glancing up at him through my lashes. His hands slipped into my hair, gripping tightly to the strands as I took the head of his dick into my mouth. I sucked lightly, taking my time as he thrust his hips forward. I gripped the back of his thigh with one hand and used the other to massage his balls as I took him further into my throat. He groaned, thrusting his hips harder, which forced me to take him deeper. I hollowed my cheeks, sucking him harder as he began to fuck my face. As saliva leaked down my chin and his hands held me in place, I took everything he gave me. I wanted to taste him on my tongue, but Lorenzo had other plans as he cleared his throat. Damon pulled out of my mouth with an audible pop. If looks could kill, Lorenzo would be dead by now.

I stood up from where I'd kneeled down in front of Damon and watched as he strutted to the bed. He sat on the edge and leaned back on his elbows, and kept his eyes trained on me. Lorenzo stood from his chair and walked over to me. Taking a hold of my chin, he ran his thumb over the bottom of my lips.

"I'd hoped I would have been the one to ruin this lipstick tonight, *principessa*." I'd almost forgotten that the lipstick was there.

"I'm sure you'll have plenty of other chances." If he lived long enough, anyway, I wasn't an idiot. I knew what he had planned for me after tonight.

He smiled at me before walking behind me. He turned me to face Damon as he unzipped the back of my dress, pushing it down from my shoulders as his lips trailed along my neck and shoulder. I slipped my arms from the sleeves and let the dress pool around my feet. My eyes didn't leave Damon's as Lorenzo's lips trailed across my skin. He made a noise of approval as his fingers traced the lines of my bra and panties. The look on Damon's face was a mix of hunger and blood lust. He didn't want Lorenzo touching me, but there wasn't much we could do in this situation. Lorenzo's fingers were graceful as he unhooked my bra, and the flimsy lace joined my dress on the floor. He wasted no time slipping off my panties as well, leaving me in just the heels. As he straightened behind me, pulling my back flush against his front, his hand trailed down my stomach to my core. He began slowly fingering me as Damon watched from the bed. How did we keep getting into these situations?

"*Fottere*, she gets so wet for you, Damon." He breathed into my ear as his fingers stroked my clit. I wished it didn't feel as good as it did.

I was glad when he removed his fingers from me and I let out a breath I didn't realize I'd been holding. I heard a groan from Lorenza and heard him suck on what I assumed were his fingers.

"She tastes even sweeter than she smells." He said, letting his hands slide down my arms. His breath cascaded over my neck and an unintentional shiver wracked down my spine. "He's hard for you, *principessa*. Why don't you go ride him until he comes in that sweet pussy of yours?"

I felt a mix of sadness, disgust, and desire as I walked towards Damon on the bed. He sat up straighter as I approached, slipping his hands on my hips as I straddled his lap. He was still so fucking hard, and I wished this was happening under better circumstances. I wanted him. I just didn't want Lorenzo as an audience.

My thoughts halted when Damon reached between us to cup my core, slipping his fingers into me at a leisurely pace. "Fuck me, Angel. Use me to make your pussy weep."

A moan slipped past my lips. Fuck, I loved when he said shit like that. So possessive and controlling. While with anyone else, some of the shit he said would just piss me off. Not Damon. His words and the feel of his hands set me aflame. Like all he cared about was me. I decided to try not to think about things too much. I wanted out of my head for a while, and Damon had always been the best way to quiet my mind.

I kissed him hungrily, slipping my hands into his hair and releasing it from its tie. I loved his long hair and gripped the strands in my hands. He continued his ministrations, fucking me with his skilled fingers and kissing me back just as furiously. His mouth captured my moans of pleasure as he worked me quickly to orgasm. I shattered, toppling over the edge so fast I lost my breath. No one knew my body better than Damon.

"That's my good little slut," He praised, removing his fingers from my cunt to position his cock at my entrance.

A whimper left my lips as he thrust upward, filling me up in one fluid motion. His hands found my hips, moving me on his hard erection. "Ride me, Angel. Make me feel that greedy cunt strangle my cock."

His name fell from my lips in a breathless moan as I began to ride him, lifting myself up before sliding back down his length. The feeling of him inside of me and the dirty words he whispered had me aching for him. If he kept that up, there was no way I was going to last very long.

His mouth found my breast as I rode him and he sucked the hardened peak into his mouth, biting just the way I liked. He knew just how to mix pain in with pleasure and my body sang for him. He moved one of his hands around to work my clit as I rode him, giving me the perfect amount of friction. I was so close to another release and from the sounds Damon was making; he was too.

"That's right, Angel. Just like that." He moaned against my chest, moving to the other nipple to give it the same attention he had the other.

We were so lost in each other that I almost didn't notice when Lorenzo came up behind me, slipping a slick finger over my backside, down to my ass. In my surprise, I stopped riding Damon as my body tensed, and not in a good way. Lorenzo pushed me forward into Damon as he got a better angle on my ass.

Damon leaned back, pulling me with him as he placed a light kiss on my lips. "Eyes on me, baby girl."

His whisper was so quiet I almost missed it. He crashed his lips onto mine and began to thrust up into me. His pace was slow, almost soothing as Lorenzo lubed up my ass, slipping his fingers into my back entrance at the same pace. I moaned against Damon's lips while my body remained tense. The only person who had ever had me like that was Damon. I didn't want this. Almost as quickly as it started, Lorenzo removed his hands from me, and I heard the deafening sound of his belt and pants being undone. Damon bit my lip, trying to draw my focus to him as he went back to stimulate my clit with his finger as Lorenzo's hands found my waist. I'm sure my face was a mix of disgust and anger. Damon was doing everything he could to keep my focus on him, regardless of the same anger burning in his eyes. At that moment, I knew that one of us would be putting an end to Lorenzo Russo.

Without warning, Lorenzo pushed into my ass. His thrusts were slow at first and he would thrust into me at the same time Damon was pulling out. I had never felt so full in my fucking life. A wave of pain and pleasure ripped through me as they both fucked me. Their massive cocks slid into me at a perfect rhythm, their dicks rubbing each other from inside of me. They both groaned out in pleasure as their thrusts slowly increased in pace.

All I could do was grab onto Damon's muscular shoulders and take what they were giving me. They were slamming into me in tandem. The sounds of wet flesh and our combined sounds of pleasure filled the room until I was screaming out my release. My vision tunneled as they continued to fuck me, filling me to a point of combusting. Another orgasm overtook me, one after the other, as I dug my nails into Damon's flesh. I watched with blurry vision as Damon threw his head back and roared out his release. His cock twitched inside of me as he filled me to the brim. Lorenzo soon followed, cursing in Italian as he filled my ass with his come. As soon as he stilled, he slowly pulled from my ass, walking over to one of the doors where he pulled out a cloth to clean himself up with. I was fucking spent as I collapsed onto Damon's chest. He wrapped his arms around me, holding me to him as if he thought I'd break. We were both breathless, and I didn't want to leave the safety of his arms.

This shit was a fucking nightmare.

CHAPTER FORTY-ONE

Damon

This shit was fucked. I had been escorted out of the fucking place as soon as Lorenzo was done with his fucking power trip. While it had been enjoyable being with Angel, I was pissed that the fucker had been the one in control of what was going on.

Angel had just lain there afterward. A blank look washed over her features. If she'd been the crying type, I'm sure she would have been in that moment. I'd taken my time to hold her while Lorenzo had left the room to get himself cleaned up, and I took care of my girl. She hadn't said a word the entire time. She'd retreated inside of herself, so I did the only thing I could do at that moment. I held her in my arms and talked to her. Hoping that at the very least, she'd been listening.

As soon as Lorenzo came back, I was told to get dressed and a group of guards walked me out the front door. Every fiber of my being was screaming at me not to leave her there, but she'd asked for a month to get herself out. I would give her that. Not a fucking day more. A part of me hoped that I'd be the one to end that sorry son of a bitch.

Dimitri, Cherry, Zack, and that little red head were waiting out front with our car. I couldn't even care fucking less that we had some slaver bitch with us. I didn't fucking care about right now other than Angel being stuck here.. All I saw was red, and killing Lorenzo Russo was the only thing on my mind.

"Don't tell me to fucking calm down!" I roared at Zack and Cherry.

They'd been on my ass since coming back from that fucked up party. Every day, they hounded me. Asking if I was okay when they arrived at the club. Dimitri had stuck close to Cherry since getting her back, so he'd spent most evenings that she'd worked sitting at the bar. He'd done nothing to stop the insistent line of questions from the twins. I was going to end up murdering them all.

"Damon, we are going to get her back. If anyone can get out of that place, it's Angel. She's been scoping out the place since she showed up. Keeping an extensive record of everything, including when guards were patrolling outside of our window. She'd checked and all the windows were sealed shut. She'll come up with some way to get out. I'm sure of it." Cherry was always so fucking positive about everything. I just didn't want to hear any of it.

I threw the keys to Hellfire on the bar in front of Dimitri and walked out. I'd ridden my bike today, and I just needed to get out of there. I'd gotten word that there were some fights going on in the next town over and I was going to need to draw some blood if I was going to be stuck fucking waiting around for the next month.

CHAPTER FORTY-TWO

Angel

I'd woken the next morning after the event in my little prison cell. Everything was sore, and I just wanted to stay buried in these blankets for the next month. Fuck this bullshit.

I didn't even remember anything after Damon had pulled me into his arms last night. I really didn't want to think about what had happened. This had been my idea. I'd taken the deal Lorenzo had offered me, so all of it was on me. Looking over at Cherry's bed, I noticed that it was empty and unused. At least she'd gotten out. That was what mattered the most. Cherry was safe and with her family again. Now I just needed to focus on surviving this hell I'd gotten myself into.

I wasn't doing shit until I could get out of my own head. I pulled the covers over my head and went back to sleep.

Three days went by where I simply stayed in bed. I didn't worry about showering and I hardly touched the food that Dante would bring me. I was thankful that I hadn't had to face Lorenzo yet. Dante had even informed me I was free to roam the house, so long as I stayed on the grounds. I was a prisoner, but one who had a leash.

I finally decided it was time to stop sulking and get a plan together. I needed to find a way to take down Lorenzo's business from the inside and get rid of him. We didn't need another him swooping in to cause problems later on down the road. It had to be clean, and we had to have someone in power that we could trust. I was sure that Jensen would know what to do once I gave him access to the information he needed, anyway.

Thanks to the notebooks they'd provided Cherry before I got here, I was able to write down everything I learned and did. I needed there to be a record in case I didn't make it out. I knew Damon would come storming this place as soon as my month was up and he'd need the information to keep things running smoothly or hand things over to Dimitri, anyway. Things could get messy fast if I wasn't careful.

I slipped out of bed and decided three days was long enough to lie around without taking care of myself. Grabbing a pair of black sweatpants and a white sports bra before heading into the shower to make myself more presentable, in case I ran into Lorenzo while I looked around. I still wanted to dress for comfort. I didn't know if I'd need to fight off some asshole in this place.

Aside from the occasional guard, the place was quiet as hell. I wasn't sure who all stayed here. I was curious if the others I'd seen at the party over the weekend were housed here or somewhere else. Brushing the thought away as I walked the halls, I took in the erotic abstract that was scattered around the place. Why did rich pricks have to flaunt their money and have these big ass houses? It seemed like a waste, considering every large house I'd ever been in was completely empty. It would have made more sense if they had a big family or some shit like that.

My search led me to find absolutely nothing of interest. Every window was sealed shut and the only exits were the front and back doors. Why couldn't shit just be easy so that I could get out quickly? I found my way back to Lorenzo's office and opened the door a crack. To my surprise, it was empty, so I slipped in, shutting the door behind me. The laptop Lorenzo always used was sitting there open on the desk, so I did the only logical thing in this situation. Once seated at the desk, I took off my watch, popped the face-off, and extracted the small flash drive. I tossed it into the slot on the computer and a countdown bar appeared, counting down from thirty seconds. While that was going, I started looking through all of Lorenzo's files. I wasn't the most tech savvy, but I'd learned a couple of handy things over the years to cover my tracks. When you spent eight years stalking and killing people, you had to learn to do certain things.

The files were all about his business. It took me a bit, but I was finally able to find something of use. I quickly opened up a secure email and proceeded to attach the files to the message just in case this drive or whatever didn't work like it was supposed to. Jensen had made sure I knew how to contact him if I was ever able to do so. There were files of all Lorenzo's contacts, offshore account information, where he held his "stock" prior to their sale, and a couple of files containing sensitive information about many of those involved in Lorenzo's unsavory adventures. After sending the email, I quickly wiped any trace that I'd been there and made sure everything was exactly how Lorenzo left it. The driver had finished doing its thing by the time I was done snooping. I took it from the computer, slipping it back into the hidden compartment of my watch. I wasn't sure if what I'd sent would be helpful for the guys, but I was confident they could figure shit out for themselves. They'd been in this business a lot longer than me and had smart people at their disposal.

Standing from the desk, I decided to see what books I could find in Lorenzo's personal collection. If I was stuck here, I might as well find something to do with my time. I'd just found a fairly interesting collection of poetry when the door clicked open. I didn't bother to look back as I scanned through the book in my hands.

Soft footsteps echoed across the floor and stopped behind me. I had to remind myself not to act out of character as I flipped to the next page. The worst thing I could do would be to act like I'd been snooping and sticking my nose where it didn't belong. Soft fingertips brushed along my arm as the other snaked around my waist, pulling me back into a muscular body. Where

Damon was rough and calloused, Lorenzo was hard muscle and soft skin. He reminded me of Dimitri in that aspect. He was clean cut and rarely got his hands dirty. Definitely not my type.

"What are you doing, *principessa?*" His soft Italian accent brushed along my shoulder.

"Looking for something to do. I'm bored and I'm tired of reading romance." I placed the book back in its spot, picking up another to flip through.

His lips brushed over where my neck met my shoulder. "Ah, so you aren't the romantic type?"

I chuckled darkly, pulling out of his arms to put the book back and face him. He was dressed in a pair of heather grey slacks, a black button-up shirt, and black leather shoes. His shirt was undone at the top to show his chest and sleeves rolled up to show off a scattering of tattoos on his forearms.

"Romance and love aren't my thing," I said, studying him to get his reaction.

He simply smiled at me, taking my chin between his fingers as he closed the distance between us. "What can I do to change your mind? I don't believe wooing you is the right way to earn your affections."

"I didn't realize earning my affection was part of your game. I'm simply a prisoner in a pretty cage."

I really needed to learn how to keep my snark to myself. His eyes hardened on me and the smile dropped from his face. Yep. He didn't like to be sassed. He slipped his hand from my chin into the hair at the nape of my neck, jerking my head back.

"I do not appreciate your tone."

He twirled me around to face the desk, pushing me over the top by my hair as he used his other hand to lower my panties and sweatpants. Lorenzo didn't waste any time pushing them down farther than he needed and a zipper being undone filled my ears. Fuck if he was going to have me without a fight.

Using my hands, I pushed off the desk and kicked my foot back, making contact with his leg. He grunted as I scurried away from him. Pulling my pants up as I went. I didn't get far. I hadn't hit him hard enough because he grabbed my ankle from his spot on the floor, pulling me down to the ground with him. I tripped, catching myself quickly, trying to kick him off me with my other foot.

He might be a softer sort of man, but he was fucking strong and pinned both my legs down, dragging me towards him. I screamed out in rage, trying to hit him with fists and nails. Once I was close enough, he used his body to pin me down and forced my hands above my head. His lips found mine as soon as he had me restrained and I bit at his lip until I could taste the coppery taste of blood on my tongue. I managed to get a hand free and raked my nails down his face, using every bit of fight I had in me.

He wasn't having any of it. A growl of warning left his chest as he pulled off of me long enough to flip me and pin my hands back over my head. On my stomach, I had no fucking leverage, and I found him hard as he ground into my ass. I tried to buck him off as he pulled my pants down again. I was fucking fucked. There was no way to use his weight against him, and from this position, his larger frame could easily overpower me.

With no warning or preparation, he slid himself into my pussy. A pained gasp left my lips as he thrust into me repeatedly. He used one hand to hold down my wrists and moved the other under me, where he stimulated my clit. The fucking bastard wasn't going to just take from me. He was going to make me enjoy it. A moan slipped past my lips as he hit me in all the right spots. My core tensed as my orgasm built. Fuck, fuck, fuck!

"Enjoy it, *principessa*. Your body loves the feel of me. I can feel that sweet pussy tightening around me. You're so fucking wet and tight like this." He whispered in my ear, never losing his pace as I came apart at the seams.

A scream ripped from my lungs, a mix of torment and pleasure. "That's it. Come for me. Soak me in your sweet nectar, *principessa*."

I felt like I'd lost whatever fight was in me. My orgasm and fight leaving my body at the same moment. I hated myself at this moment as Lorenzo fucked me. Bringing me pleasure and my own special brand of pain. My nails dug into the hardwood floor as he continued to thrust into me.

If I couldn't stop things like this from happening, I might as well learn to end things as quickly as possible. Using what renewed strength I had, I pushed back. Meeting his thrust with my own. While my mind was screaming at me that this was wrong, my body wasn't on the same page. I'd enjoy what I could and do my best to take down Lorenzo's empire from the inside. I imagined all the ways I'd enjoy killing him. Moans left my lips as he stretched me, filling me. His own groans of pleasure filled my ears. If only he knew that my moans were over the scenes I played in my head where I tortured him, fileted him like a fish, and bathed in his blood while he begged for mercy.

CHAPTER FORTY-THREE

Angel

Things were so fucking weird. Once Lorenzo was finished with me, he turned back into that charming persona he wore. He took his time to care for me and clean me of our combined fluids. Looking him over as he did, he looks so disheveled. His pristine hair fell out of place over his right eye and a small trail of blood trailed down his chin where I'd bitten his lip. Deep scratches marred his face where I'd been able to dig my nails into his skin. I took pride in the fact that he wasn't walking away from this incident without a scratch.

Once he was satisfied that I was clean, he insisted on carrying me back to my room, where he drew a bath in the oversized tube filled with lavender-scented bubbles and proceeded to wash my hair. I had no fight left in me at this point other than the burning desire to make him pay before this was all over. He was kind and caring as he washed me, which just fucked with me more. When he was finished washing my hair and body, he surprised me by undressing and getting into the tube behind me. Before I could protest, he pulled me back into him, fitted between his muscular thighs. I could feel him hardening again against my back as he pinned me to his chest.

"I'm aware this isn't what you wanted, but I want to make you happy." He said into my hair.

"You want to own me." I was seething.

"*Sì*, I want to own you. I want you to belong to me and only me. However, I want you to enjoy your time with me as well. Do me the honor of at least trying to be open-minded about your situation. I can take care of you and give you everything you could ever want in this life."

I didn't justify his statement with a response. I couldn't bring myself to. The chains binding me to this man just kept getting tighter. The more I fought, the tighter they'd become. In 28 days, Damon would be here or I'd be dead.

"Let me please you, *principessa*," he whispered, trailing kisses over my neck and shoulder.

It was time to get out of my own head and play this how it needed to be played. Emotions were getting thrown out the window and I would do what I needed to do. I leaned back into his touch, a light moan slipping from my lips.

I felt him smile against my skin as his hand found its way between my legs. I opened them wider for him as his fingers ran down my slit. In my head, I could imagine it was Damon's fingers instead. The thought had me moaning loudly in pleasure as he slipped two fingers into my warm center. His skilled fingers worked me ever closer to the edge. Before long, I was rocking my hips into his hand. He whispered praises in Italian against my skin as he moved his fingers faster, curving them to hit that soft flesh inside of me that had me screaming out my release.

CHAPTER FORTY-FOUR

Angel

Two weeks had passed and every morning I awoke to tangle in the sheets of Enzo's bed. He'd been insistent that I move into his room. The room itself was 3 times bigger than the one he'd had Cherry and me in. It was decorated in black and grey with accents of gold throughout. He had 'my belongings' moved into his walk-in closet, which was bigger than my old apartment, and the bathroom housed an oversized jacuzzi and a waterfall shower.

Slipping out of the bed, I made my way into the bathroom to shower and get myself ready for the day. I'd been spending the past few weeks snooping as Enzo allowed me more freedom to explore the grounds. Taking note of the guard shifts and where they were stationed around the grounds in the surrounding wooded areas. I needed to get as much information to the guys if they were going to succeed in taking over Enzo's business. I hadn't been able to send what I'd found yet, but I was making sure to keep an accurate mental note of everything they may need.

When I wasn't snooping, I was requested to accompany Enzo in his office or room, where he took his time in bringing me to orgasm. Every time he touched me, I had to imagine it was Damon instead and scrub myself raw in the shower until I felt halfway clean again. A part of me had to admit he was skilled in how he used my body, but it just didn't feel right. It hadn't been the first time I'd used my body like this. As if my sexuality were my own personal weapon, but it was the first time I had feelings for a man while sleeping with someone else. It was just wrong on so many levels. This is why I tried to stay as far from other people as possible. Caring about someone led to nothing but trouble and heartache.

After showering and getting dressed in a red sundress and black flats, I made my way down the hall to do some more exploring. Before I could really get anywhere though, a throat cleared behind me. Turning, I found Dante heading my way. What the hell could Enzo's bitch want now?

"*Il Capo,* would like to see you." He said before leading me to the office I'd become very acquainted with over the past few weeks.

I didn't say anything as I followed him. I'd learned really fast that opening my big mouth only had it being gagged or filled. I wasn't interested in having Enzo force his dick down my throat again. It took days to get the taste of him off my tongue.

I walked into the office ahead of Dante and Enzo waved his hand to dismiss him. He really was a little fucking bitch. He did whatever Enzo told him to do. Without looking back as the door was shut behind me, I walked over and sat on the edge of the desk next to where Enzo was typing away on his computer.

"You wanted to see me, Enzo?" I asked, running my fingers lightly over his exposed forearm. Play the part, Angel. That's all you have to do, I reminded myself.

He glanced at me over the rim of his glasses before taking them off to lay on the desk, "*Sì,* you have been on your best behavior these past few weeks so I wanted to take you out of the house for a little while."

I smiled at him, my fingers stopping their light track on his arm. "What did you have in mind?"

He flashed me that charming smile, showing off his pearly white teeth, "It's a surprise."

Surprise probably wasn't the best choice of word. This view was the most beautiful thing I'd ever seen. Enzo had wrapped up his work for the day and then drove us out to the docks where a large yacht awaited us. Now that I thought about it, I was sure we were only a few miles away from where Doc had put that tracker in my neck. The throat had me rubbing at the spot where he'd stabbed me and I could just feel the device underneath the skin embedded in the muscle underneath. I shook my head to rid myself of my thoughts as I made my way onto the boat with Enzo leading the way. The thing was completely decked out with lights and romantic Italian music playing over the sound system, and the crew set sail out into the open ocean.

There was nothing for miles as we continued to sail across the sea. The sunset on the water was breathtaking, and I simply sat at the front of the ship watching as the sky turned into golden colors. It was peaceful and I couldn't help that my mind continued to wander to Damon. What was he doing right now? Was he watching the sunset now too? I'd become a love-sick teenager when it came to him. A part of me still revolted at the idea, but if I wasn't going to be around much longer, the least I could do was stop lying to myself. Even if I did lie to everyone else.

"*Questo tramonto non è nemmeno paragonabile alla tua bellezza, principessa.*"

I jumped, spinning around to see Enzo walking up to me. He was dressed casually in a pair of nice khaki pants and a button-up white dress shirt that had the top three buttons undone and his sleeves rolled up. He was attractive, but something was lacking. I couldn't ever imagine myself feeling for him like I did for Damon.

I rolled my eyes, turning back to look at the view. "Will you continue to talk to me like that when I have no clue what you're saying?"

He sat down behind me and pulled me into his embrace, watching the sunset with me. "This sunset does not even compare to your beauty, princess."

He whispered the words against my skin as his lips trailed along my exposed neck where I'd thrown it in a messy bun earlier in the evening. I leaned back into his touch while my stomach did flips, and not in a good way.

"I'm never going to figure out what you're saying," I said as his lips trailed down to my shoulder.

"You will learn, *principessa.*"

"I've been trying for weeks and still don't understand any of it." I huffed and shrugged him off my shoulder.

He simply chuckled and pulled me back into his chest. "We will discuss it further later. For now, let's enjoy our time together." He trailed his hands down my sides, to the front of my sundress, lifting the hem up my thighs slowly, "Would you care to dance with me, *principessa*?"

"I don't dance." My body felt tense, like my skin was too tight over my body. A suffocating feeling washed over me at Enzo's touch. Why couldn't this shit be simple? I just had to go and catch fucking feelings for someone. Fucking stupid.

Enzo stood, taking my hand to pull me up with him. The man was charming and graceful. I would give him that. He took his time leading me to the center of the deck, where there was plenty of space to dance. He spun me like I'd imagine someone spinning a ballerina before pulling me flush against his chest, one hand holding mine and the other delicately placed on my waist, "You've never had the right partner."

The dance was slow and sensual, going along perfectly with the soft music playing from the speakers that ran the length of the boat. I just followed his lead as he spun and turned me. I wasn't used to giving this much control to someone else. Even with Damon, there had been a sense that I had a say. With Enzo, it was all how he wanted things to be. He was at the wheel and I was simply along for the ride. Could I find comfort in my new situation for however long it would last? It was doubtful. Some way, somehow, one of us would end up six feet under.

CHAPTER FORTY-FIVE

Damon

The crowd roared as my fist met my opponent's face, bone cracking beneath my knuckles on impact, and blood flew from his mouth. He fell to the floor, KOed, as the "ref" did the whole counting thing before lifting my hand in the hair while the audience cheered. Money was passed around, the smell of blood, sweat, alcohol, and smoke filling the air of the warehouse we were in.

These weren't legal fights, so the crowd was a mix of bigwigs looking to gamble away their fortune and scum alike. I ripped the tape from my hands as I left the loud cheers and blaring music for the silence of the empty locker room. The smells were worse here as I worked to rip the lock from my locker and take a swig from my water bottle. I needed a fucking drink.

This had been what I'd done every night while I counted down the days to either get the call that Angel was back or for me to storm that fucking place and get her out. I was hoping she'd make it out on her own, but it had been weeks. I'd heard nothing about her from Dimitri or Jensen. Last they knew, she was perfectly fine and still locked away in Lorenzo's mansion. She'd gotten the drive installed and now Jensen had access to everything. Dimitri was working on getting the big things handled and looking into replacing Lorenzo with someone in our pocket. We couldn't leave things to chance again. It was better to be a part of the business, no matter how much we hated it, but Dimitri was positive he could find someone to take the seat who would do as we said. No more stealing girls. No more forcing people into these situations. It would only be those who were interested in offering their services with well-planned out contracts that benefited everyone involved.

The sounds of music and cheers rang through the room as the door to the locker room was pushed open and in sauntered a pretty blonde in a suggestive outfit and heels. She smiled at me as she walked over, getting into my space. It took everything in me not to knock her skinny ass to the ground.

"What?" I snapped. I wasn't interested in what she had to offer or in wasting my time.

"Hey there, handsome. I was hoping you'd like to hang out tonight." She smiled, dragging her long-ass manicured nails down my bare chest.

"Not interested." My voice was clipped as I backed up a step, reaching into my locker to grab a t-shirt and tossing it on. If the bitch touched me again, I didn't trust myself to not start swinging.

The blonde seemed surprised that she'd been turned down. She tried to reach for my arm, but I was much faster, wrapping my fist around her slender arm and twisting until she whimpers in pain. Fear flashed in her big brown eyes, but I didn't care as my anger burned through me.

"Get out," I growled between my teeth, pushing her away from me. I didn't even have the energy to care as she scurried from the locker room.

Without a word to anyone else, I threw my crap in my bag and headed out, jumping on the back of my bike and heading back to Angel's apartment for the night. I'd been staying there since she'd been taken. The place still smelled like her lavender and lilac scent, and it was the only place that gave me a sense of calm while everything else was going to shit. My life was in chaos with Angel here.

The worry was eating me alive while all I could do was sit here and wait.

I showered, throwing my wet hair up into a bun, and lay in the bed. Images of Angel during our moments together flashed through my mind as I lay in the darkness of her apartment. My hand found its way around my cock, working the length as I hardened at the thought of her. Heard her sounds of pleasure in my head. I imagined she was riding me right now, her head thrown back in ecstasy as her cunt strangled my cock. It didn't take me long to come all over my stomach, groaning her name as I found my release.

Soon. I'd have her back soon.

CHAPTER FORTY-SIX

Angel

We had spent the past five days on the boat. Exploring small island areas off the coast and taking a swim whenever we were anchored, and the sun was too hot on deck. I found myself forgetting my worries as the days passed and I was floating in the soft waves. Almost forgetting what my purpose had been for all of this. I wasn't Angel or a captive in a pretty prison for a moment.

The weather had been perfect. Warm with a slight ocean breeze and not a dark cloud in sight. The evenings were cooler, which made the evening dinner on deck perfect. The crew handled all the heavy lifting and a private chef prepared all of our meals. This left me with all the time in the world to pretend this was the type of life I'd always wanted. I'd forced myself into a sense of denial about my situation. Choosing to live in fantasy for as long as possible.

Enzo groaned from his spot between my legs. His tongue gliding over my clit in the aftermath of another orgasm that left me breathless. I moaned out his name, my fingers tangled in his hair. He'd made sure to let me know I was to moan out his name. The thought had me wanting to roll my eyes, but it was better to just get it over with instead of arguing about it. We'd been spending so much time in this bed that I'd lost track of everything he'd done with me. I'd found myself enjoying his touch more and more over the past couple of days. My body craved the release he offered and the haze of an orgasm. It was just another way to get out of my head for a bit. Afterward, I still felt dirty, wishing I was with Damon again.

His lips trailed to my inner thigh, which I knew held the scar of Damon's brand, "I wish you'd have this covered up, *principessa.*"

I propped myself up enough to look at him, plastering a teasing smile on my face. "Why do you have to ruin the moment like that?"

He crawled up my body, forcing me to lie back down as he positioned himself over top of me. I could feel his hard cock pressing against my entrance as I opened my legs wider for him. His lips found mine in a passionate kiss, our tongues colliding in a show of dominance. It wasn't filled with need and hunger like my kisses had been with Damon. I missed *that* sort of passion, but this could work. At least the sex was enjoyable, I guess.

It didn't take Enzo long to slide into my slick entrance. My walls clenched around his length as he thrust into me at a leisurely pace. His movement was precise as he continually hit that sweet spot. He enjoyed drawing out my release.

"Please, Enzo," I thrust my hips, needing more than he was giving me. I craved a rough fucking, but that wasn't his style. Sex was a dance, and he enjoyed getting me to that edge just to deny me. Where Damon tortured me with orgasms, Enzo denied me. Forcing me into a needy mess before he'd give me what my body needed.

His lips trailed down my jaw and throat, down to my breast, where he took one into his mouth. Sucking and biting at my hardened nipple. I moaned out his name as a plea. Begging for release. My nails dug into his back as he pushed me further toward the edge of blinding pleasure. All that could be heard in this small cabin were the sounds of skin hitting skin and my moans of pleasure as he slowly worked me up. He'd get me right there and then change his movements just enough to piss me off.

I grew tired of his games, using my strength to flip us over so that I was on top. Lifting myself and upping the pace. I fucked him hard and rough. Just the way I liked and needed it. Trying my best to pretend as if it were Damon's cock I was bouncing on.

His hands found my hips, his head tilted back as he groaned out in pleasure. Curses in Italian flew from his lips as I forced us both over the edge. My orgasm barreled into me so quickly my vision blurred and I lost myself in the bliss. His cock pumped up into my tightening cunt as he chased his own release. My name tumbled from his lips as he filled me. I collapsed on the bed next to him, trying to catch my breath. Our combined orgasms coated my thighs and a slight ache was apparent at my core.

In the moments afterward, I really hated myself. I hated that I enjoyed fucking Enzo. Hated myself because I had wished it had been Damon's come sliding down my legs as I made my way to the private bath where I'd shower away the evidence of what had just occurred. I couldn't stand to look at myself in the mirror anymore. I barely recognized myself anymore.

What the hell had I become over the past 22 days? Just 9 more days and this would all be over.

CHAPTER FORTY-SEVEN

Angel

Six Days left. That was all the time between now and when Damon would come.

Following the trip out on the yacht, we returned to Enzo's in a blissful sort of mood. He'd informed me that he'd be hosting another event in three days, similar to the one he'd taken me to prior. He told me things would be a bit different this time around, but he'd give me the details later.

I was happy to remain blissfully unaware of what there was to expect at another one of these events he liked to have. Hoping that I wouldn't have to see Damon at this one. I wasn't interested in him seeing me as this shell of a person I once was. One that bent to the will of her capture and didn't put up a fight. I couldn't stand to look at myself in the mirror most days because the disaster that looked back wasn't Angel anymore.

The days prior to Enzo's event were a blur of tangled limbs, searching around for any other useful information, and lots of scotch. Scotch was the only way I found to cope, and it reminded me of the taste of Damon. He had scorched his mark on my body and soul. He hadn't just branded me; he owned me. I was royally fucked.

Today was the big day. A group of women came in to see that I was prepared for the event to Enzo's specifications. They took their time getting my body washed and then slathered in creams and oils. They tried different hairstyles and makeup looks to make sure everything was perfect while I sat silently in a silk robe, nursing a crystal tumbler of scotch. If I had to go to another one of these fuckfest events there was no way I was doing it sober. I was really surprised however when they didn't dress me in a gown. Instead, they left me in nothing but a black lace thong, my black silk robe, and a pair of red bottom stilettos. This didn't bode well for me, but I was just drunk enough not to care.

When they were finished, they'd settled on my hair being left down in long waves, a simple smokey eye, and a bold red lip. If I made it out of this, I would never wear this color lipstick again. As they were finishing cleaning up their supplies, the doors opened and in walked the man of the hour.

He was dressed in black slacks with a baby blue dress shirt. The sleeve rolled up, as usual, to show off his muscular forearms and tattoos. I'd realized soon enough that he didn't have nearly as much ink as me. His tattoos were small and scattered across his arms. Outside of that was simple bare skin. Not once had I had the desire to trace the art with my tongue. It wasn't even remotely as enticing as the ink that covered Damon from neck to toe.

I really needed to stop thinking about him so much.

The women scurried out of the room with their supplies as Enzo walked up to me, taking a strand of hair between his fingers as if admiring the soft ringlets. "You look stunning, *principessa.*"

"Thank you, Enzo." As I drank from my glass, I smiled at him over the rim. I was already slightly drunk and my words sounded slurred, even to my own ears. I must have had more than I thought.

Enzo wore a look of annoyance as he took the tumbler from my hands and sat it out of my reach. "I need you to be on your best behavior tonight. You have an important part to play tonight for our guests, so don't be sloppy."

"You still haven't told me what my role will be." I glared up at him. He really pissed me off when he wasn't making me come.

"You'll be the main attraction tonight. A treasure to be seen and unable to be touched. I want every man and woman in attendance tonight to crave you." His fingers trailed along my jaw until he held my chin in his hands. This had been his power move with me since the beginning, and I had to fight the urge to snap my teeth at his fingers. "You're mine and I intend to make that known to everyone this evening. My own personal toy to do with as I please."

His words sent my blood boiling. I didn't have a say in any of this, but it explained the lack of clothing. He intended me to be a show like the other people he sold at these events. He wanted to use me to gain more profit. The hornier he could get the crowd, the more money they would be willing to spend on the others that they *could* get. I nearly rolled my eyes.

He didn't explain much more as he led me downstairs to the same doors as before. The sound of music and voices flowing into the hallway. I was glad that I'd drank enough to be slightly out of it. Though it made walking in these ridiculous shoes a bit harder. I had to grip tightly to Enzo's arm to keep from falling. Enzo released his hold on me and I stumbled slightly. He gave me a cutting look, which had my spine straightening as he stood in front of me. From his pocket, he pulled out what looked like a collar attached to a chain.

What in the actual fuck was that for?

He slipped the strap of black leather around my neck, fastening it quickly as I stared at him wide-eyed. He couldn't be fucking serious. Taking the chain in his hand, he yanked me towards him, forcing our bodies as close as they could be. "You will be my obedient little pet tonight, *pincipessa*. Just behave and put on a good show for all of our guests."

He loosened his grip on the chain, allowing me the space to back up a step. "Now slip out of that robe for me."

I hesitated a moment before pulling the string that held my robe together. The silk fabric glided over my skin as it fell to the floor around my feet. I set my shoulders back, trying to maintain some sort of dignity. At least that's what I told myself.

"Good girl, now open that pretty mouth."

This time there was no point in hesitating. I opened my mouth as he gripped my face while pulling a ball gag from his pocket. I guessed he didn't want me mouthing off in front of his *friends* tonight. He slipped the ball into my mouth and fastened it behind my head. He looked at me as if in praise for following his orders as he stood back to look me over.

"*Così bella.* Now on all fours. I want them to watch you crawl."

I did as he instructed. Sliding onto my hands and knees as he nodded for the guards to open the doors. He pulled on the chain, leading me into the room full of people in pretty gowns and expensive suits. I watched the floor as I crawled after him. If there is a god, please don't let Damon be here to witness this. If he saw me crawling like this, I'd set this whole fucking building in flames with myself locked inside the inferno.

He led me through the crowd, towards the front of the room, up a short set of stairs that lead to a raised stage area. Looking up through my lashes, I saw a bench that had an area for arms, legs, and a head to go. I had to assume it was a sex bench, because why wouldn't it be? He led me over to it, where he pulled on my leash, ordering me to stand.

I tried my best not to look at the faces of the gathering crowd as he moved me to take a place on the bench. The leather of the bench was cold to my skin as he strapped me to the thing, forcing me to have my ass in the air for all to see. I still wore the lacy thong, so that was a plus for now, I guess. My neck, wrists, and ankles were all restrained in leather belts as my hair fell down around my face, almost hiding me from the view of the crowd.

Enzo began speaking, but I couldn't hear a thing that was said. My heart was hammering in my ears, so I closed my eyes tightly with my head resting on the cushioned headrest of the bench. It wasn't long before I felt Enzo's hands on my hips.

"Be a good girl, *principessa*." He said, ripping the flimsy lace from my body, exposing my pussy and breasts to the crowd.

As if I had a fucking choice. He took his time running his hands over my ass before walking away for only a moment. What felt like soft leather replaced his hands. If I had to guess, it was a riding crop you'd see used at horse races. Enzo trailed the crop down my spine, down to my ass where he began to whip me with it. I tensed as the blows landed on my ass, whimpers leaving my open mouth from the sting. From this angle, I could already feel saliva running over my lips and chin. This shit was humiliating and my dumb ass was just taking it.

This time, the crop didn't land on my ass like I'd been expecting. It connected with my pussy. A moan fell from my lips as my fists clenched, pulling against my restraints. I was going to kill him.

This *punishment* continued for what felt like hours, but I was sure it was only a few minutes. Once the lashing stopped, I heard a belt being undone before Enzo slammed his cock into my throbbing center. I couldn't even enjoy it as he pounded away at me. Making a show of his prowess. I was sore from the crop and I was positive at this point that the nerves in my pussy had been numbed from the lashing. This wasn't meant to be pleasurable like my other times with him. Why did men think that pounding into a wet hole somehow made them more of a man? To me, it just seemed pointless and showed that they didn't know how to please a woman.

Enzo groaned as I felt him fill me with his come. The evidence leaked down my thighs onto the bench beneath me as he pulled out. A cheer rang through the crowd as I listened to him refasten his pants and belt.

"I hope you all enjoyed this little demonstration, as she will be open to paying participants for the evening, for your pleasure. I will advise that you steer clear of her mouth. This one has a bit of a bite. *Gustare!*" Enzo chuckled, giving my ass a final smack as he descended the stairs into the crowd.

What the fuck did he just say? I lifted my head, watching as he was patted on the back and handed checks from men in the crowd. This fucker had just sold me like a fucking piece of meat. I pulled on the restraints, trying to loosen them so I could get the fuck out of here. Scanning the crowd, my eyes landed on the face of Dimitri. A panic washed over me as I looked around to see if Damon was next to him. Thankfully, it seemed as if Dimitri had come alone. I was sure it had to do with their contract that he had to attend this fucking thing. I almost sighed in relief, knowing that Damon wasn't here to witness my *fall from grace*. Dimitri excused himself at that moment, slipping from the room and pulling his phone from his pocket as the door shut behind him.

The first man to ascend those fucking steps was a bald, muscular man. He looked like a bodybuilder in a fucking suit. As he made his way over to me, he tossed his suit jacket onto the table that housed all sorts of whips and toys. He ignored them all as he walked behind me and a nearly deafening sound of his pants and belt hitting the floor filled my ears. He grabbed my hair roughly, pulling my head back as much as he could with the restraint around my neck as he slammed into me. Tears stung my eyes as he fucked me with no remorse. His grip on my hair tightened as groans of pleasure came from him until he was exploding inside of me.

This treatment continued. Men took turns filling my pussy and ass for their own pleasure as my tears and saliva ran down my face. Come leaking from me, creating a mess on the bench. My knees slid on the wet leather, and the only thing holding me in place were the belts that wrapped around my neck and limbs. No one cared to clean me up after they were done. I lost count of the men after fifteen. They just kept lining up like I was some sort of fucking prize.

At some point, I must have blacked out. I blinked my tearful eyes to see the room empty and Enzo leaning in front of me, where he removed the ball gag and unfastened my restraints. Everything hurt and my limbs felt heavy. All I could do was watch him numbly as he removed me from the bench, cleaned me up with a damp rag, and carried my limp body up to the room we'd been sharing.

The last thing I remembered before my world turned black was him lightly tracing my shoulder and back with his fingertips.

"You did so well tonight, *principessa.*"

I awoke to the sound of Enzo talking in a hushed tone. Opening my puffy eyes, I saw it was still dark in the room and Enzo was standing by the open window, talking on the phone. He hadn't noticed I'd woken up, so I simply pretended to sleep and listened to his conversation. It was a mix of English and Italian, but I understood enough to gather what the conversation was about.

Jensen must have gotten my messages because from the sounds of things, Enzo's organization was crumbling. I could hear the anxiety and anger in his voice as he told whoever was on the other end of the line to get things fixed.

"Gabriele, get this mess cleaned up… I don't give a shit if it's impossible. Figure it out, *imbecille.*" Enzo hung up the call before sliding back into the bed behind me.

He wrapped his arm around me, pulling me back closer to his front.

Two more days and this crap would be over.

CHAPTER FORTY-EIGHT

Damon

"It's almost time to go in and get her. She's been sending Jensen information on and off for the past month on top of him being able to hack the systems. She even gave us detailed time stamps of shift changes for the guards in and around the estate. We have everything we need to take down his operations, and I've sent teams out to take care of anyone who may try to step in. We've contacted the man who we are appointing in Lorenzo's place and he's on our side." Dimitri said while looking around the dingy locker room.

"Is she still alive?" I asked, unwrapping my bloodied hands.

Since I'd walked out of Hellfire almost a month ago, I'd been spending all my time fighting in underground fight rings. I'd made a good amount of profit from the matches I'd been winning, and the violence was something I needed to keep from storming into Lorenzo's place to get my girl back. I was wound tight, just waiting to hear something. Any sign that she was okay or that she needed me. I knew she didn't need me to save her, but this waiting was killing me.

"Her last message was sent two days ago. Now, can we leave this filthy place already? I'm going to have to burn this suit." Dimitri sounded absolutely disgusted. He'd always been a pompous ass and a neat freak. I did notice pity washed over his face for a moment when he mentioned hearing from Angel a few days ago. He was hiding something, but I wasn't in the mood to push.

"Yeah, let me just grab my shit. It's time to go get my girl."

Everything was in place as we parked down the road from Lorenzo's estate. A group of men had been sent out to get rid of the guards so that we could make our way in without anyone being able to warn their boss. I didn't need that fucker making his way out with my girl. She would be mine again before the sun came up in the next few hours.

My fists clenched in anticipation as I sat there with my men, waiting for the green light. It felt like I'd been sitting here for days when it had only been about ten minutes. I lit another cigarette, doing anything to keep myself busy. What was taking those idiots so fucking long? Sitting in this SUV, I was going to start popping off my own men if they didn't hurry the fuck up.

"All clear, sir." One of my men said over the comms.

"You heard the fucker move out." I nearly yelled at the driver.

He didn't take offense as he put the car in drive and drove us through the gates of the estate. My men stood there ready to open the gate as we drove through. Once we were through the gates we jumped out of the car and made our way up the long drive surrounded by its own little forest on foot. We used the trees and bush for cover as we made our way up to the front of the house. My personal explosives guy was already working to rig up the front entrance as I made my way over to a hiding place behind a large oak tree.

"Detonation, in ten seconds. 10, 9, 8, 7, 6, 5, 4, 3, 2…"

A loud explosion shook the ground as the door was blown off its hinges. Without wasting a second I rushed into the building. Shooting any of the guards who fired on us. My men followed me inside the foyer as we took out Lorenzo's men. It was the perfect image of destruction as dust and gunfire filled the air.

I almost rushed towards Angel as I saw her being led away from the action by Lorenzo and his right-hand man. She was dressed in a casual set of black leggings and a cropped top. From here, I could make out bruises across her body, despite her tattoos. I wanted to rip those clothes from her body and see just what damage that fucker had done to her. Her eyes snagged on mine before she turned to the man at her side. She made quick work of throwing a right hook and elbowing him in the gut. As soon as he doubled over, she grabbed his gun, firing a round into the guy before pointing it at Lorenzo.

CHAPTER FORTY-NINE

Angel

Everything was in complete chaos tonight. Smoke and gunfire filled the air as Lorenzo and Dante led me through the front room. Lorenzo was shouting orders in Italian over his earpiece, not paying any attention to me. Stealing a glance at the front door, I could see Damon opening fire on anyone who stood in his way as he forced himself into the mansion. His eyes met mine, and a fire engulfed me from that simple look.

I glanced away long enough to see an extra gun inside of Dante's holster and I knew exactly what I'd need to do. As fast as I could, I rounded on the man, throwing my fist into his chin in an uppercut, elbowing him in the stomach, and grabbing the gun before he knew what had hit him. Just as fast, I unleashed bullets into him as his body crumpled to the floor and a puddle of blood began to form under him on the grey floor. Fuck, I'd forgotten how good it felt to be in control of someone's life like this. I quickly took out any of the guards within range as Lorenzo turned to face me with wide eyes.

I wasted no time at all pointing the gun at him. "Tell your men to stand down."

The shock morphed into anger as he did as I'd instructed. There were few men left standing as the foyer had turned into a war zone. Damon's men quickly took out the rest as they unarmed themselves, and all that was left was an eerie silence.

"Was this what you'd been planning all along, *principessa?*" He asked as he glared at me.

"Not exactly. I didn't plan on living this long," I said as I walked closer to him.

"*Avrei dovuto sapere che sarebbe successo quando eri così facile da controllare.*"

"You know, I always hated when you'd talk to me like that," I said, tilting my head to the side.

Lorenzo simply smiled as Damon made his way over to stand at my side. His men went off to search the rest of the grounds for any loose ends. Lorenzo still stood as confident as ever. I didn't understand what he had to be confident about. He'd just lost, but he just smiled that charming smile of his. I didn't like this. Something was wrong and I could feel it in my gut.

"Are you alright, Angel?" Damon asked, taking the gun from my hands.

"What took you so fucking long?" I glared at him as he pointed his gun at Lorenzo's head. His lips turned up in that crooked smirk that I had missed these past weeks. He was covered in blood and damn if it didn't do something for me.

"I wouldn't celebrate so quickly. Things just got interesting." Lorenzo's smile turned wicked right before a gunshot was heard from behind us.

Pain ripped through my back and chest as I fell towards the floor. Fuck. I glanced around as my vision began to blur around the edges to see Dante with a gun pointed at me.

"I tried to warn you, *principessa*," Lorenzo said, as he pulled a gun from his back and pointed it at Damon.

It was getting harder to breathe, and I could feel the blood dripping from the corner of my mouth. The metallic taste filled my mouth as I coughed up more of my own blood. I didn't even think as I pulled a dagger from Damon's leg holster and launched it at Dante. It hit him square in the arm, causing him to drop the gun he'd been pointing at Damon. The last thing I heard was gunfire as my world faded to black.

CHAPTER FIFTY

Damon

My heart stopped as I watched my girl fall to the floor, a steady puddle of blood forming around her body from the bullet wound. How she managed to throw that knife to disarm Lorenzo I had no clue, but I needed to act fast.

As swiftly as I could, I aimed my gun at the dying man on the floor, shooting him in the head. He slumped to the floor, finally dead, as I rounded on Lorenzo. A quick death was far too nice of an ending. I wanted him to suffer, especially if anything happened to Angel. A blind rage overtook me as I thought about Angel and I launched towards the fucker, tackling him to the ground as my fists met his face. He tried to fight back, but it was a useless battle. All I could see was the blood and hear the sounds of bones cracking. My knuckles ached, but I couldn't stop even as the man beneath me stilled. The rage had taken over as my fists connected one after the other.

I wasn't sure how long I spent beating him. It could have been minutes or hours. I didn't stop until hands wrapped around me, hauling me off that piece of shits body as I fought to punch his face through the fucking floor. Things didn't come into focus again until my brother stood before me and slowly his and Zack's voices filtered in through the blinding fog that had taken over.

"That's enough, brother. Let's focus on getting Angel out of here. She'd lost a lot of blood and isn't looking good. We have to get her to the doctor." Dimitri said, holding me in a steel gaze.

Looking over, I found Zack and a medic looking over Angel. Her pale skin was ghostly white as they hooked her up to all sorts of machines to check her vitals. Without asking for permission, I walked over, scooping her into my arms to rush us out to the waiting van.

"If he's not dead, detain him for me. I want him fucking alive." I spat, rushing out the door to get my girl to the doctor. Fuck, she just had to be okay.

CHAPTER FIFTY-ONE

Angel

Everything hurt. My head felt like someone had split my head open with an ax. It even hurt to breathe as I blinked my eyes open to the white-washed ceiling, where ugly fluorescent lights shone brightly. Who turned the fucking lights on so damn bright and where the hell was I?

Trying to sit up, an intense pain shot through me, stealing the breath from my lungs as I fell back onto the uncomfortable as fuck bed I was in. My mind was drawing a blank of what was going on and I was pissed that even the slightest movement had me in so much pain.

"Glad you see you awake, baby girl."

That voice. I'd know that voice anywhere. My eyes cut to the side to see Damon leaning against the door frame, a bouquet of red roses in his hand as he smirked at me. My face must have shown my surprise as he prowled into the room, filling the small space with his muscular frame.

Flashes of him storming Lorenzo's place flashed in my mind, the sound of the gun going off before I fell to the floor. I winced as the memories replayed in my mind. My mouth was dry and scratchy as I tried to speak. My tongue felt like sandpaper and as if my tongue filled my mouth, leaving me unable to make a sound.

Setting the roses on the bedside table, Damon reached for a cup of water, bringing the straw to my lips to drink, "Slow, Angel. You've been out for a few weeks."

Once I'd had enough water to unstick my tongue from the roof of my mouth, I looked up at him, glaring. "I hope you weren't worried about me."

I still ached as I fought the pain to sit up. Like hell if I was going to be stuck in this fucking bed. I groaned in pain as I took in my body. My chest was wrapped in gauze and a hospital gown of some sort hung around my waist loosely. As if they hadn't wanted to cover up the bandages in case they needed to get to them.

"I was terrified I'd lost you." Damon whispered as he sat on the edge of the bed, which dipped under his weight.

I scoffed, rolling my eyes. Just because we admitted we cared for each other didn't mean we had to do all that lovey dovey shit. That just wasn't who I was. "It'll take more than a fucking bullet to take me out."

Damon smirked, the gesture not reaching his eyes. For someone so big, he was a fucking softie sometimes. Worry laced his brow as he took my hand in his, kissing the knuckles. In doing so, I saw his knuckles wrapped in bandages, taking in the cuts that marred his perfectly tattooed skin. He looked like he'd been through hell and hadn't been sleeping, if the dark circles under his blue eyes were any indication.

"What happened to Enzo?" I asked, just above a whisper. I hoped he was dead.

For the first time, a true grin graced his kissable lips, "I'll show you once you get out of here."

I didn't like the answer, but didn't have the energy to fight him. With a sign, I laid back down, giving my body the time to recover. How long would it take for this shit to heal and why was it so painful to breathe?

"What exactly happened to me?" I asked, not daring to look at the man sitting next to me as I stared blankly at the ceiling.

"That bullet went through your lung. You were nearly dead once I got you to Doc. He worked hours to keep you alive. For five days, you were on machines that breathed for you before you started breathing on your own again." His deep voice was rough like gravel as he recounted what had happened after I was shot. Purposely skipping over anything about what had happened to Enzo.

No wonder I felt like shit, and it was just about to get worse.

"Damon, I need Doc to run some tests for me." I avoided his gaze as I pulled my hand from his.

"What happened, Angel?" His voice was so calm. Goosebumps broke out along my arms. That was the voice of a man out for blood. But that blood belonged to me.

CHAPTER FIFTY-TWO

Damon

It took everything in me to stay seated as Angel recounted the things that were done to her the night she was sold, as if she were nothing but a fucking sex toy. I wasn't sure how I managed not to go on a rampage once Angel had fallen asleep.

My little Angel. So battered, and yet she didn't let that bring her down. There was no regret or remorse on her face. No shame in what she'd been through. Only a deep rage that burned in her cold steel eyes. How could someone remain as strong as she did with all she'd been through in her life? She was a force that was strengthened by all the disaster that followed her throughout her life and she continued to fight. Thriving in her darkest moments.

Using everything done to her as a way to harden her own armor.

When I was sure she would be sleeping the rest of the night, I left the room. A calm washing over me as I made my way into the hall. I needed to make a phone call. My girl would get her revenge and I'd revel in watching her burn the world to the ground as she collected the blood she was owed.

Stepping outside, I lit a cigarette, letting the smoke burn my throat and lungs as I made some phone calls. I'd find out every single person who placed their filthy hands on my girl. They'd regret ever being born when she was finished with them.

CHAPTER FIFTY-THREE

Angel

They made me stay in the fucking hospital for another week, running a shit ton of tests, and having me speak with a counselor before they would discharge me. All the tests came back clean despite how many fuckers had stuck their filthy dicks in me during that "party". I tried not to think too much about all that.

It had been interesting talking to the quack, at least. She must have been new, because when she looked over my file, she seemed to admit about me seeing a therapist regularly. I'd made it clear it wasn't going to happen. I'm sure that took some strings being pulled by the boys, but I didn't care. Only one thing was going to make me feel better. Letting the blood of those fuckers paint my skin to hear their screams of pain. I wasn't sure how I'd find them, but I wouldn't stop until every single one of them died at my hands.

I still had a long road of recovery, so I had plenty of time to make the necessary plans. Until then, Damon and Cherry fussed over me. Cherry was a sniveling mess when Damon dropped me off at my old apartment to rest. The little group from Hellfire was there to welcome me back, including that pretty redhead who'd been on display at the first event I'd gone to with Enzo. I'd been thankful when Damon ushered everyone out for me to rest.

After two weeks of being taken care of, I was over it. Throwing on a pair of sweatpants and a tank top, I left the apartment while Damon was showering. It felt good to feel the wind against my face as I drove through the city on my bike. I'd left my phone and a note on the bedside table, so Damon wouldn't burn down the entire city, hopefully. I was already expecting a lecture, so I stayed out until well into the night.

By the time I made it back, I was ready to collapse in my bed again. Pulling up, I was surprised to see an array of nice vehicles in the parking lot. That couldn't be a good sign. Everyone was in my apartment when I walked through the door.

Cherry launched herself at me, wrapping her arms around me in a tight embrace that left pain shooting through my chest.

"Oh my god, Angel! We were so worried about you! Where were you? Are you okay?"

Prying myself from her grip, dragging in a lungful of air that left me wincing as I made my way to the counter to pour myself a shot of whiskey. I was hurting after my day out and I needed something to numb that feeling. One wasn't going to be enough, so I threw back 2 more before I looked at the group of people in the small space. If they were all going to keep coming around, I'd need a bigger place than this shitty studio apartment.

"Everyone out." Damon said in a deathly calm voice, never taking his eyes off me.

Cherry was about to protest until Dimitri placed a hand on her lower back to lead her out the door. Zack following close behind. If they were all here, who the hell was working at Hellfire, anyway? Looking between the bottle and shot glass, I decided maybe it was useless to dirty the glass. Tipping back the bottle before I made my way to the bed, reclining against the headboard to relax. The air was tense as Damon watched my every move. A calm before the storm settling over us. I took another swig before cutting a glare in his direction.

"I left the note, so there was no reason to cause a scene. I was fine."

Anger flashed in his eyes as he stalked towards me, his large hands gripping the railing on either side of me as he towered over me. If he was trying to intimidate me, he'd have to do better than that.

"Shut the fuck up, Angel." A growl sounded deep in his chest, sending a wave of heat to my core. All I could do was smirk, taking another drink from my bottle.

"I'm fine." I seethed through my teeth.

His hand lashed out, gripping my chin as we glared at each other. "You will stay in this bed until you are completely healed. I'm not going to risk losing you because of your stupid ideas."

"You don't fucking own me, Damon." Anger filtered into my voice, sounding like a hiss.

Damon's fingers dug into my skin as his lips crashed against mine. He engulfed me in his heat as our mouths battled for dominance. A clash of tongue and teeth as his hand moved down to my throat, the other tangling in my hair as he consumed me. The way this man tried to dominate me made my blood boil. Anger and lust mixing in a toxic combination, leaving me breathless and hungry.

I wasn't sure how it happened, but Damon's mouth traveled down my body, biting in places, leaving a maddening ache in my core as my pants were ripped from my body. His hands were roaming, but never touching where I needed as I gasped for air. Catching my breath was still a challenge, but I couldn't bring myself to stop him as he delved between my thighs. His tongue flicked that bundle of nerves until I was moaning out his name. My fingers tangled in his long hair as I chased my own release. I was so close already, my pleasure building as he slammed his fingers into my core, sucking my clit into his mouth in the perfect rhythm.

"Oh god," I moaned, nearly choking on the lack of air filling my damaged lungs.

He didn't stop until I was coming on his tongue and finger. A silent screaming left me as my body tensed. Fuck. What the hell did this man do to me?

He lapped at me as I came down from the high, wincing as the air filled my lungs again. He watched my every move as his tongue traced the mark he'd left on my inner thigh. A challenge gleaming in his eyes.

As soon as I could breathe again, I pushed a foot against his chest, forcing him away from me as I got up and locked myself in the bathroom. I was starting to think that fighting with him was a losing battle.

CHAPTER FIFTY-FOUR

Damon

Angel was finally getting back to normal after her eight weeks of recovery. She'd been hell to deal with. Not wanting to stay in bed to actually rest. A few times I'd even resorted to cuffing her to the bed. The only thing that kept her sated was promising her pleasure.

Just the thought had me aching to fuck her, but she wasn't ready for that yet. I'd been counting down the days until I could sink balls deep into her warm cunt. Waiting for Doc to give me the okay. Today was that day, but I had plans for her first.

My girl was currently in the shower, getting ready to go out today. I'd told her I had plans for us, but she didn't know exactly what my little surprise was. I lounged on the sofa, flipping my knife in my hand as I waited for her to walk out the bathroom door.

The water cut off and after a few moments; she was strutting out that door in a pair of low-rise, skin-tight jeans, a black crop top, and her leather jacket. Her hair was a wet mess around her beautiful face and it took everything in me not to take her right here and now. My cock straining against the zipper of my jeans.

"Well, let's go." She rolled her eyes, heading straight for the door, and I followed close behind her. Steering her towards my bike as we walked outside.

"Is this necessary? I have my own." She asked, crossing her arms over her chest with a glare in her eyes.

Ignoring her comment, I threw my leg over, handed her a helmet, and started the bike. The rumble of the engine vibrating through me. "Get your fine ass on this bike. Now, Angel."

She huffed, but did as she was told, climbing on the bike behind me. As soon as her arms wrapped around my waist, I took off. Heading towards Hellfire.

CHAPTER FIFTY-FIVE

Angel

He still wouldn't tell me what the hell we were doing at Hellfire as he led me through the dark main floor. His hand wrapped tightly around mine as he led me towards the back and down the stairs to the basement. Who the hell did he have down here this time?

The place was silent as he unlocked the door to one of the rooms, flicking on the overhead fluorescent lights. I couldn't see shit until he stepped from in front of me, showing the view of a very familiar man dangling from chains attached to the ceiling.

My eyes widened in shock as I took in the shape of the one and only Enzo. He was out cold, but breathing. His face and body were a bloody mess. No longer looking to be the powerful man he'd been before all this. He was at the mercy of someone else now.

Damon moved, tossing a bucket of water on the battered man before me. "Wakey, wakey."

He taunted as Enzo came too with a jerk; the chains rattling with the movement. He seemed surprised when his eyes landed on me standing in the door. I could have sworn I saw fear wash across his face for a moment and I felt a wicked smile grace my lips.

"I've been working on getting names for you, Angel." Damon spoke, stepping in my line of vision, his hands lightly grazing over my arms as I looked up into his deep blue eyes. "This is your fight. All their lives are yours to take. So I've saved this asshole for you and collected the names of the others."

I felt tears burn the backs of my eyes. He wouldn't take this from me. Keeping Enzo alive for me to deal with and collecting the names of the men who'd been forced on me. He'd just handed me the best gift anyone ever had. My heart swelled, and a smile graced my lips.

"Him we save for last. Let's get to work."

I took my time going through the list. Taking out each person who'd taken part in the shit show at Enzo's estate. Taking my time to humiliate and ruin each person's life before ultimately disposing of them. In total, there had been thirteen of them. I didn't know how many had been involved. My mind clouded the event in an effort to protect me from the things they'd done to me while I was chained down like a rabid animal. Blocking out all that shit had probably helped me from spiraling, that's for sure. Now I could relish the feeling of holding their lives in my hand. Damon never interfered in any of it. He got me the names and information I needed while I took care of the rest.

Now there was just one more person left.

Enzo hung from the chains still in the basement. Covered in blood and his own filth. Given just enough to stay alive until I was ready for him. Tonight would be his last on this earth, and I wanted to savor every moment of it.

Hellfire was closed, and I locked the doors behind Lily and Cherry as they left for the night. Damon sat at the bar, a tumbler of his favorite scotch in his hand as he watched me. I hadn't told him what my plans were, but he knew tonight was the night. Tossing my things onto the counter next to him, I made my way down to the basement, Damon following closely behind me.

CHAPTER FIFTY-SIX

Damon

My dick was hard as I followed Angel down to the basement. My eyes focused on the sway of her hips as she walked into the room where Lorenzo was being held. I loved watching her work, taking out every shred of anger on the men who'd hurt her. Fuck. She was beautiful in her element.

The door to the room swung open, Enzo hanging from his chains and the smell of filth and decay filling the air. He didn't deserve any comfort after the shit he did to my girl. Selling her off to anyone willing to pay him. If this weren't Angel's kill, I'd make him suffer.

I closed the door behind us, taking a seat in the metal chair next to it, straddling the frame and leaning forward on the backrest as I watched my girl look over an array of toys lain out for the night. I hadn't been sure what she wanted to do, so I added a little of everything on the counter.

Enzo was silent, watching her with fear shining in his eyes as she ran her hands over the knives and weapons in front of her. Her hand eventually wrapped around the hilt of a boning knife. A wicked smile spreading across her pale rosy lips. She hadn't been wearing her normal red lipstick since coming back. I found it best not to ask her about it, even though I missed the color.

"Damon, care to go get me some salt and lemons from upstairs, please?" She asked without looking at me.

I stood, going upstairs as she took the knife in her hand, shredding the clothes from Lorenzo. I would gladly bow at her feet if she'd asked me to. The confidence she normally wore bleeding out of her and she started working on the flesh of one of Lorenzo's thighs. His screams filled the air until the basement door shut behind me.

I rushed to the bar, grabbing the things she'd asked for before going back down. The man's leg was in tatters. The flesh hanging from his thigh in odd places, other pieces littering the plastic on the floor beneath him. Curses in a mix of Italian and English spilled from Lorenzo's mouth as he jerked against the chains holding him suspended in the air.

"Hold still. I wouldn't want you to bleed out before I've had my fun." Her voice came out through gritted teeth as she fileted the man like a fish. It reminded me to never get on her bad side, though the thought of being at the mercy of her blade made my cock ache as it pressed against the zipper on my jeans.

Content to simply watch, I sat the lemon wedges and bowl of salt on the counter next to her before taking my seat again. Resting my chin on my forearm as I watched to strip the flesh from muscle and bone until he was nearly skinned alive. The sight was gruesome, but seeing Angel covered in blood made me feel savage. The glee in her eyes shining as the fucker screamed and begged for mercy as she worked.

"How are you keeping him awake?" I asked as she stood back to admire her handy work.

"Gave him some amphetamines before this." She said simply, tilting her head to the side as if in thought.

She flipped the blade in her hand once before stepping over to him again, taking his chin in her other hand as her thumb ran along his bottom lip. "You have such a beautiful mouth, Enzo."

A sly smile spread across her lips. Enzo's eyes widened in shock as she brought the blade to the corners of his lips, slashing it across his cheeks in a permanent smile. He yelled out in pain as blood dripped down his chin to his chest, thrashing against the restraints as she walked over to the counter, tossing the knife onto the countertop, and poured a handful of salt and lemon juice into her palm.

I smirked as she walked back over, taking his damaged face into her hand, forcing the mixture into his fresh wounds. The sounds of gagging pain filling the air once more.

"Oh, shut up. You know, it wasn't so hard to get all the information on your business and find someone else to take over in your place. Someone who would follow our orders on how things would work from now on. Gabriele was happy to be of assistance." Enzo was glaring daggers at her now as her fingers pressed into the bloody gashes along his face. "Everything you worked for crumbling to the ground and being taken over by the people you hate most. It's too bad you'll never get to see it."

She pulled a blade I hadn't noticed from her back pocket, using it to saw his flaccid penis from his body before shoving it down his throat. He gagged, thrashing once again as he choked. Struggling to breathe as she held his mouth closed with her hand, nails digging into the bloody flesh until he became still. Only 53 seconds and he'd died from asphyxiation.

She backed up from his body, shedding the bloody clothes she wore before turning to face me. Blood covered her pale flesh, her tattoos and the blood standing out as her shoulders relaxed. Sauntered over to me, she slid her hands into my hair, which I'd left down tonight, as she brought her lips to mine. Kissing me with a new sort of hunger. Slipping my hand around her throat, I stood, pulling her where I wanted her as my tongue explored her mouth. Hot and needy as our tongues fought for dominance. Pressing her back against the door, I moved my hands to her thighs, lifting her so that I could grind my jean covered cock against her soaking folds. God, I could feel the heat through the thick material, feel the wet spot forming against me.

"Take out my cock," I ordered, trailing my mouth along her jaw, down her throat. The taste of her sweat and blood filling my mouth as she reached to undo my pants.

As soon as my cock was free, I slammed into her waiting cunt, groaning out in pleasure as her warm heat surrounded me. I wasn't soft or loving at that moment. I fucked her ruthlessly until she was screaming. Her head hitting the door with every thrust of my hips as she held onto me. Nails and her heels digging into my back until she was coming on my cock.

"Mine," I growled into her ear, causing her pussy to spasm around my length.

"Shut up and keep fucking me."

Her order was breathless, and she didn't have to tell me twice.

CHAPTER FIFTY-SEVEN

Angel

I was so fucking tired. I'd lost count of how many times Damon had fucked me once I'd finished off Enzo. First in the same room as Enzo's body hung there rotting, then on the floor, in the shower, in the car, in this very bed we lay in once we'd made it back to my apartment.

Now I was wrapped in his arms, a tangle of limbs as we lay there trying to catch our breath while I rested my head on his broad chest. Groaning when he sat up, moving me from my comfortable spot. I just wanted to rest so I could ride his cock. I was insatiable and wanted more of him. Things had been off for too long since getting better. This was actually the first time we'd actually had sex since everything went down. Other than him eating me like his last meal, we hadn't been doing anything else.

Damon moved from the bed and I watched that fine tatted ass as he walked over to his pants by the couch. My core clenched in want as I watched him move to pull something from the pocket, tossing the jeans back onto the floor before walking back over to the bed. My eyes snagged on his hard dick as he stood at the foot of the bed. I still couldn't see what he had in his hand as he used the other to pull my leg until I was on my back, legs spread wide as he climbed between them, taking a place there as he placed an open box on my belly. I stared wide-eyed at the ruby red ring that starred up from the little jewelry box, gasping when he flicked my clit with his tongue.

"Damon, what the fuck is this?" I asked, trying to sit up.

His large hands gripped my hips to hold me down to the bed. "Marry me."

It wasn't a question as his tongue slipped into me, fucking me at a fast pace as my hands tangled in his hair.

"Fuck," I moaned out, my thoughts about the ring shattering as he lapped at my core, sucking my aching clit into his mouth.

For a moment, I forgot what he'd just said as my world shattered and I came on his tongue. Damon wasn't done with me yet as he reached to move the box from my stomach before flipping me over onto my hands and knees, slipping easily into me from behind. His hand found its way into my hair, yanking my head back as he pounded into me.

"Answer me, Angel." He growled. Enunciating every word with a hard thrust.

"Yes." I couldn't form any other words as he plowed into me, another orgasm building in my core. Fuck. What had I just said?

CHAPTER FIFTY-EIGHT

Angel

"I can't believe you actually said yes!" Cherry squealed as she gushed over the ruby that now graced my ring finger. It was a silver band, wrapped in diamonds, with a large ruby stone in the center glistening under the lights of the bar.

"Don't remind me." I used my right hand to take another shot as we sat at the bar of Hellfire. Cherry still hadn't let go of my hand as she looked over my new engagement ring. Even I couldn't believe that I'd said yes when Damon asked.

I'd admitted my feelings for the asshole and I'd stuck around after healing from my gunshot wound. Yeah, that shit hadn't been fun. It was hard to believe everything that had happened. The gunshot wound, the recovery, taking out all those men, and finally getting to end things last night with Enzo. It felt like a weight had been lifted. Like I could finally have a life.

"Need another shot, Angel?" Lily asked from behind the bar.

She'd been the pretty redhead from the first party Enzo had taken me to. Zack had outright bought her that night to get her out of there. She hadn't had a place to go, so she stuck around. She was a sweet girl, and she'd been a big help with things at Hellfire. Zack was wrapped around her finger, and it was nice to see him so happy.

"Please," I handed her my empty glass as Cherry finally released my hand.

"Don't let her get too drunk. She still has work tonight." Damon said from behind me.

"On second thought, I'll just take the bottle." I reached over the counter and snatched up the bottle of scotch before turning to face my soon-to-be husband. I wasn't sure I'd ever get used to that.

He was smirking at me, a fire in his eyes as he looked over my body. I took the stopper out of the bottle and tipped it back. Chugging a good bit of it before hopping up from my stool.

"Yeah, about that boss, not happening. I'm calling out sick." I made my way up the stairs to the VIP lounge, knowing that Damon wasn't far behind me.

Walking in, I plopped down on the soft sofa and took another swig from the bottle, watching Damon walk in and shut the door behind him. He almost prowled towards me. A hunger in his eyes, as if he were stalking his prey. I just smiled at him and offered him the bottle once he was standing in front of me.

Taking the bottle from my hands, he placed it on the coffee table and pinned me to the sofa. His hand wrapped around my throat as he forced me to lie back, making himself comfortable between my legs.

"What am I going to do with you, my little Angel?" He growled, before capturing my lips with his in a tangle of tongue and teeth..

I kissed him back, slipping my hands into his long hair to pull him closer to me. Him mixed with the taste of scotch, was euphoric. I couldn't get enough of him, of his touch. I was his completely regardless of how much I tried to run from those feelings. And he was just as much mine as I was his.

Angel Ashford. It had a nice ring to it.

EPILOGUE

Today was the big day. Everything was decked out in black and red. No white in this wedding, because I wasn't innocent in the slightest. It was a small affair, with just our close friends, to witness something I never would have seen in my future.

Cherry and Lily were currently fussing over my hair and makeup. I'd agreed to let them doll me up after weeks of them bugging me about it.

"Can I look yet?" I was currently sitting here with my eyes closed while they worked, refusing to let me see until they were finished.

"Just one more thing." Cherry giggled, applying something to my lips. My heart leapt into my throat. The thought of lipstick left me anxious, even after months of working to get my shit together. I found myself hoping that it wasn't the bright red lipstick that had once been my favorite.

"Okay, now you can look." Lily's sweet voice echoed in that southern accent of hers.

With nerves fluttering in my belly, I opened my eyes and looked towards the mirror. My jaw nearly dropped as I looked at my reflection in the mirror before me. My hair was up in an elegant curly bun atop my head, stray curls falling around my face. The eye makeup was light, with a natural brown smokey eye, black wing liner, and glamorous false lashes. The colors made my eyes appear almost a cool silver. What caught my attention was the lipstick Cherry had applied. It wasn't the bright red I'd loved, but a deep maroon that I immediately loved. It wasn't my usual, but I had to admit a part of me had missed the confidence my choice of lipstick used to give me.

"I know why you don't wear your red lipstick anymore, but I thought this would look perfect and more like you." Cherry said, standing next to me.

I felt the burn of tears, but refused to let them fall as she wrapped her arms around my shoulders, joining me in the mirror.

"You look beautiful, Angel." She whispered.

"Thank you."

I was still choked up as the girls helped me step into my black lace wedding dress. It was all lace, appearing as if there was nothing underneath, with long sleeves that fell just past my wrists. It fit like a glove, the back plunging just above my ass. The fabric flaring out behind me. A perfect mix of elegant and dark.

Lily handed me my bouquet of black and red roses, which I nodded as a thank you before they left to take their seats. My heart raced, beating against my chest until it ached. Only worsening as the music began to play. That was my cue. Damon had rented a small beach house with a private beach. A ramp leading directly to the waves that crashed on shore.

With a deep breath, I made my way out the back door and down the ramp. Our small group of friends seated before an archway decorated in black tulle and roses. My eyes couldn't take any of that in, though. Not when all I could see was the man standing there waiting for me. His hair was tied up in his usual bun, his beard was styled and trimmed, and he was in an all black suit with a rose red tie.

I barely registered my feet moving until I was standing in front of him, Cherry taking my bouquet, and him taking my hands in his. He pulled me close, one hand slipping around my waist so that we were nearly pressed together.

The officiant did his thing, walking us to the part where we say I do. I couldn't help but to shift on my feet as he said the words I wasn't sure I was ready to hear.

"You may now kiss the bride."

Damon's deep blue eyes stared at me as his fingers slipped into my hair, angling me just the way he wanted.

"You will always belong to me, Angel." He growled, lips nearly brushing mine.

My breath nearly hitched at his words. We'd danced around this plenty of times before. I'd made sure he knew I didn't belong to anyone.

"Yours.

Also by Hayley Briana

The Hellfire Series

Angel of Blood

Angel in Chains

Sweetest of Fires

Hellfire

Fires of Damnation (coming 2024)

Darkside Fairytales

Belong to Me

All Mad (coming 2024)

Be My Guest (coming soon)

On the Hook (coming soon)

Haunting Series

My Dark Haunting

My Dark Terror

My Dark Dolly

My Dark Ending

Haunting

Fall Series

Fall From Grace (coming 2024)

Fall to Sin (coming soon)

Love Me Series

Love Me in the Dark

Love Me in the Moonlight (coming soon)

About the Author

Hayley Briana is an indie author currently residing in Colorado. As a mom & wife, she finds herself in need of some major self-care in the form of a good cup of coffee (or wine) and a good book. Escaping into a world of fantasy is Hayley's favorite pass time outside her day-to-day responsibilities. When she's not adulting or writing, you can most likely find her tucked away in her home library.

For more info on Hayley and what she is working on please visit HayleyBrianaWrites.com

Follow Hayley on Social

Instagram.com/hbrianawrites

TikTok.com/@beautyandthebookcase